# EARNIN' A LEARNIN'

Fargo caught himself against the wagon wheel. He tasted blood on his mouth where the sucker punch had landed. He looked through narrowed eyes at the man who had struck him.

The dandy called Bart stood there, fists clenched, face red with rage. "That's twice you stuck your nose in my business, and now I'm gonna teach you a lesson for it!"

Fargo straightened. Bart's friends were still behind him, but no one was hurrying to Fargo's side. In fact, most of the townspeople were backing off.

Except for Maddie. She stepped forward, saying, "Get away from him, you—"

"Shut up, whore," Bart said with a sneer as he shoved her back.

Fargo wiped the blood off his mouth. He glanced at the crimson smear on his hand, but that didn't bother him nearly as much as what Bart had said and done to Maddie. "You said something about teaching me a lesson. Well, come on, boy." He raised his hard fists as a cold smile came over his face. "I'm ready to go to school."

# THE TRAILSMAN

## #245

# BLOODY BRAZOS

**by**

**Jon Sharpe**

A SIGNET BOOK

SIGNET
Published by New American Library, a division of
Penguin Putnam Inc., 375 Hudson Street,
New York, New York 10014, U.S.A.
Penguin Books Ltd, 80 Strand,
London WC2R 0RL, England
Penguin Books Australia Ltd, Ringwood,
Victoria, Australia
Penguin Books Canada Ltd, 10 Alcorn Avenue,
Toronto, Ontario, Canada M4V 3B2
Penguin Books (N.Z.) Ltd, 182–190 Wairau Road,
Auckland 10, New Zealand

Penguin Books Ltd, Registered Offices:
Harmondsworth, Middlesex, England

First published by Signet, an imprint of New American Library,
a division of Penguin Putnam Inc.

First Printing, March 2002
10  9  8  7  6  5  4  3  2  1

The first chapter of this book previously appeared in *Pacific Polecats,*
the two hundred forty-fourth volume in this series.

 REGISTERED TRADEMARK—MARCA REGISTRADA

Printed in the United States of America

PUBLISHER'S NOTE
This is a work of fiction. Names, characters, places, and incidents either are the
product of the author's imagination or are used fictitiously, and any resemblance
to actual persons, living or dead, events, or locales is entirely coincidental.

# The Trailsman

Beginnings . . . they bend the tree and they mark the man. Skye Fargo was born when he was eighteen. Terror was his midwife, vengeance his first cry. Killing spawned Skye Fargo, ruthless, cold-blooded murder. Out of the acrid smoke of gunpowder still hanging in the air, he rose, cried out a promise never forgotten.

The Trailsman they began to call him all across the West: searcher, scout, hunter, the man who could see where others only looked, his skills for hire but not his soul, the man who lived each day to the fullest, yet trailed each tomorrow. Skye Fargo, the Trailsman, the seeker who could take the wildness of a land and the wanting of a woman and make them his own.

*Northern Texas, 1860—Hell lurks
in the Cross Timbers, and gunfire echoes
through the dark valleys of the Palo Pinto Hills. . . .*

# 1

O'Bar, Texas, looked like a nice, quite little town, Skye Fargo thought as he guided the Ovaro down the wide, dusty street between the buildings of the settlement.

Less than ten seconds later, a man came sailing through the batwings of a saloon to land facedown in the street right in front of Fargo's horse.

Fargo reined in, his lake-blue eyes narrowing. The Ovaro moved back a pace as the man who'd been thrown out of the saloon rolled over and groaned.

The saloon was a squat building constructed out of chunks of red sandstone. Instead of a plank boardwalk, it had a stone walk in front of it, with a wooden awning above supported by poles that were made from the peeled and sanded trunks of saplings. The roof was shingles of red slate. A sign attached to the awning proclaimed that the place was called the Red Top.

As Fargo watched the man in the street try to push himself to his feet, three men shouldered through the batwings onto the stone walk in front of the Red Top. They were laughing, and Fargo figured they were the ones who had pitched the gent out of the saloon. The one in front was the youngest, not much more than twenty, with curly blond hair under a flat-crowned black hat that was pushed to the back of his head. He wore a black vest over a white shirt, black leather sleeve cuffs, and tight black whipcord trousers over high-topped boots. A black gun belt was strapped around his hips, and the Colt that rode in the holster had ivory grips.

Fargo had seen the young dandy's like too many times in his life. He wasn't surprised by the coarse laughter or the smirk on the man's face as he turned to his older, more roughly dressed companions and said, "Did you see the way ol' Horace went flying through the air, boys? I swear, if he'd've flapped his arms, he would've taken off like a bird!"

The other two laughed as if they knew it was expected of them. Then one of them nodded toward Fargo, drawing the younger man's attention to the fact that someone was watching them.

The young man looked at Fargo, seeing a well-built stranger in buckskins and broad-brimmed brown hat, and asked, "What are you staring at, mister?"

*A cruel, spoiled horse's ass,* Fargo thought. But instead of answering the question, he said, "You've had your fun. Leave the old man alone now."

The smirk disappeared from the dandy's face and he stiffened. He didn't like being challenged. Fargo knew this confrontation had the makings of trouble. At the moment, he didn't particularly care. He hated cruelty in all its forms, and if that meant a ruckus with this dandified youngster and his toadies, then so be it.

Before that could happen, however, one of the young man's companions put a hand on his arm and said quietly, "Come on, Bart. You know we got places to be."

For a moment, Fargo thought the young man was going to shake off the restraining hand. Then he nodded grudgingly and muttered, "Yeah, right." The grin came back. "You got lucky, mister," he said to Fargo. "I got better things to do right now than teach you a lesson."

Fargo didn't say anything. His policy generally was to let fools think whatever they wanted to as long as they didn't cause problems for him. He had long since passed the point where the opinion of a no-account young wastrel mattered to him.

The three men moved along the street while Fargo swung down from the Ovaro and looped the reins over the hitch rail in front of the saloon. He stepped over to the man who was still struggling to get up and took hold of his arm. Fargo lifted the man to his feet with ease.

"You all right?" he asked.

The man probably was middle-aged but looked older. He had the watery eyes and red nose of a drunk, and judging by the smell that came from him, he sweated whiskey. "Th-thanks, mister," he said. "People d-don't usually stick up for me like that."

The man's hat had come off and fallen in the street. Fargo picked it up and handed it to him. "What happened in there?" he asked, nodding toward the Red Top.

"I . . . I asked Bart if he'd buy me a drink."

"And he and his friends decided to have some fun at your expense instead."

The man looked down at the ground. "If I'd let 'em kick me around a mite, they would've bought me a drink when they was done."

Fargo's mouth tightened under the close-cropped black beard. He hated to see a man whose dignity had been obliterated like this.

Someone else came through the batwings, and a woman's voice said, "I'll take care of Horace, mister. You don't have to trouble yourself."

Fargo looked over and saw a tall, slender blonde in a red gown. She was young and pretty. Frontier life hadn't honed all the softness out of her. Not yet. She came toward Fargo and reached out to take Horace's arm. The drunk's watery eyes took on a doglike devotion.

"This fella's a friend of yours?" Fargo said. He wondered if the old man was her father.

"We sort of look out for each other," the young woman replied. "Isn't that right, Horace?"

"Yes, Miss Maddie."

She said to Fargo, "I'm Maddie Jenkins."

"Skye Fargo."

A smile curved her full lips. "That's a nice name. A little unusual, but nice. What brings you to O'Bar?"

"Just passing through on my way to Fort Worth. I thought I might stop and have a drink."

"Go on inside," Maddie Jenkins said, angling her head toward the Red Top. "Tell the man at the bar Maddie says the first round is on her."

"Will that mean anything to him?"

"It should. I own the place." She smiled at Fargo.

"Much obliged."

"Horace has got a cabin on the edge of town," Maddie went on. "I'll see that he gets home all right, then I'll be back."

"I'll be looking forward to that," Fargo said honestly.

Maddie led the old drunk away. Fargo stepped into the

3

saloon, which was cool and dim inside, especially since he was coming in from a hot, bright, Texas summer afternoon. There were only a few customers in the place: a couple of townies, and three men in range clothes who probably rode for one of the spreads in the area. These rolling, wooded hills northwest of Fort Worth were good cattle country, although a few farmers were moving into the area, too. Several cottonwood-lined creeks meandered through these parts, and the rich soil of the bottomlands would support many different crops.

Not that this stretch known as the Cross Timbers was completely civilized. Far from it. Kiowas and Comanches still wandered over this way and raided from time to time. Almost a dozen years earlier, the army had built a fort down on the Trinity River, and the presence of the soldiers had pacified things somewhat, enough so that the army had abandoned Fort Worth as a military post and moved on west to build other forts. The town that had grown up around the fort was still there and was well known as one of the wildest settlements in Texas. So this part of the frontier was no different than any other: It took folks with a good deal of sand in their craw to live here.

Fargo moved over to the L-shaped bar on the left side of the room and said to the stocky man behind it, "Whiskey. And Maddie said for me to tell you that the first round was on her."

The bartender grinned and reached under the bar. "That means to give you the good stuff, not the panther piss we make with strychnine and rattlesnake venom."

Fargo returned the man's grin as the bartender poured a shot from an unlabeled bottle into a relatively clean glass. Fargo tossed back the drink and nodded in appreciation.

"Where'd Maddie go, anyway?" the bartender asked.

"She was helping some old man named Horace to his cabin."

The bartender made a face. "Yeah, when she left out of here I thought that she was probably going to get mixed up in that. I didn't hear her running off those troublemakers, though."

"They had already left," Fargo said shortly, not wanting to get into his part in the incident. "Is Maddie related to the old man?"

"Nope. She's just the sort who takes care of stray dogs and drunks. Softhearted, you know. You wouldn't think that somebody like her could run a saloon, but she does a good job of it. Want another?"

"As long as it's from the same bottle."

"Sure." The bartender poured the drink.

Fargo sipped this one and asked, "How'd she come to own this place?"

"It was her husband's, before he got himself kicked in the head by a mule and killed. He had just brought Maddie out here from St. Louis. Folks figured that after he died, she'd pack up and go home, but she didn't. She stayed on, said she was going to make a go of the place. So far, she has."

Fargo nodded, glad that the bartender was the talkative sort. He had found out quite a bit about Maddie Jenkins in a short time.

He nursed the drink until Maddie herself came back into the Red Top a few minutes later. She walked over to the bar, smiled at Fargo, and said, "I see you took me up on the offer of a drink."

Fargo drained what was left in the glass. "That was my second one, actually."

"Well, then, you'll have to pay for it. I appreciate you helping Horace, but business is business, you know." Her grin took any sting out of the words.

Fargo chuckled. "Sure." He reached in the pocket of his buckskins and took out a coin, dropped it on the bar. That almost cleaned him out, but he expected to find work in Fort Worth, and he would reach the bigger settlement that night if he pushed on.

Maddie took him by surprise by asking, "Are you hungry?"

Come to think of it, Fargo was. He had gnawed a piece of jerky at midday, but that was all he'd had to eat since early that morning. "I could eat," he allowed.

Maddie looked at the bartender. "Tell Jimmy out in the kitchen to rustle us up a couple of steaks and some potatoes. And we'll want some coffee."

The bartender nodded and said, "Sure."

Maddie took Fargo's arm. "Come sit with me at one of the tables."

5

Fargo hesitated. "I'm not sure I've got enough cash to pay for a hot meal."

"You already paid for a shot of whiskey. That comes with food and coffee."

"Is that the usual deal, or a special?"

"Like I told you, it's my place," Maddie said. "I can do whatever I want."

He enjoyed the warmth of her hand on his arm, and as they turned toward the tables and her breast pressed briefly against his side, he felt a quickening inside him. He had been on the trail for quite a while, but it wasn't just that he had been without female companionship for a spell. Maddie was smart and pretty and evidently had a kind heart. He would have been attracted to her no matter how long it had been since he'd had a woman.

They sat down. Fargo took off his hat and placed it on the table. "So where are you from, Skye Fargo?" Maddie asked.

"All over," he said.

"And where are you going?"

"Same place," he replied with a smile.

Maddie laughed. "I should have known. Some men you can just look at them and tell they're the restless sort. That's you, Skye. How long do you play to stay in O'Bar?"

"I don't plan to stay at all," he said, giving her an honest reply, the only sort he knew how to give. "I figure I'll ride on down to Fort Worth. How far is it from here, fifteen miles or so?"

"That's right." Maddie frowned. "You might be better off spending the night here and waiting until tomorrow to ride on."

Was she inviting him to spend the night with *her*? Fargo wondered. It was entirely possible, he decided. He could read the eyes of a woman just like he could read a trail, and he saw wanting in the eyes of Maddie Jenkins. Was what she was feeling strong enough for her to act on it? He didn't know, and only time would tell. It was up to him whether or not to spend that time. . . .

A bald man in an apron came out of the kitchen behind the bar carrying two plates of food, and the bartender followed with a pot of coffee and some cups. The meal arrived at the table, postponing Fargo's pondering of Maddie Jenkins and what she wanted or didn't want. The two of them dug into the food, which turned out to be quite good. Fargo washed down bites of steak with gulps of strong black coffee, just the way he liked it. Maddie ate with a hearty appetite, which Fargo liked, too. He had never cared for women who picked at their food.

"This is breakfast, for me," she said. "I'm afraid when you run a saloon you get into the habit of sleeping late. It's probably like working in a whorehouse in that respect."

Fargo lifted an eyebrow, surprised at the bluntness of her comment.

"Not that I've, uh, ever worked in a whorehouse," Maddie went on. "O'Bar doesn't even have one. I hope you're not disappointed."

"Nope. Not a bit."

"I shouldn't rattle on so. It's just that we don't get many people passing through here."

Fargo supposed that was true. Except for that flurry of potential trouble when he first rode in, O'Bar was living up to his initial impression of being a sleepy little place. Maddie Jenkins had been used to the hustle and bustle of St. Louis, so living here must have been quite an adjustment for her.

"Well, I'm glad I stopped—" he began, but before he could continue, frantic hoofbeats thundered in the street outside, and a man let out a yell. Fargo muttered, "What in blazes?"

Everyone in the saloon rushed to the windows and the door to see what the commotion was. Fargo peered over Maddie's shoulder and saw a large freight wagon hurtle past, being pulled by a team of runaway horses. A man lolled at the edge of the seat, seemingly in danger of toppling off and falling under the wheels at any moment. Fargo saw a bright flash of blood on the man's forehead.

He also caught a glimpse of the reins dangling between the pounding hooves of the team. The man on the driver's seat wouldn't be able to retrieve them, even if he hadn't been half senseless from some sort of accident.

Fargo didn't waste time thinking about the situation. The runaway wagon was already past the saloon and racing down the street out of O'Bar. Fargo stepped past Maddie and went to the hitch rail. In a flash, he had jerked the

Ovaro's reins free and was in the saddle, turning the big paint horse.

"Skye!" Maddie called after him.

Fargo didn't look back. He heeled the Ovaro into a gallop and sent it racing after the wagon.

The street narrowed to a rutted road at the edge of town. It went down a gentle slope to a half-mile-wide valley through which a creek meandered. The banks of the creek were dotted with live oaks, post oaks, and cottonwoods. Fargo spotted a narrow wooden bridge spanning the stream. Chances were the stampeding horses wouldn't be able to negotiate that bridge without the out-of-control wagon plunging off into the creek. Fargo had to stop it before it got there if he wanted to save the man on the wagon.

The deep-chested Ovaro ran with a smooth, strong gait that ate up the ground and cut into the wagon's lead. Hatless, the wind whipping his thick black hair, Fargo leaned forward in the saddle and urged the horse on. He drew closer and closer to the wagon and started thinking about how he was going to stop the runaway team.

As he came even with the back of the wagon, he kicked his feet free of the stirrups and leaned over in the saddle, reaching for the vehicle's tailgate. His fingers clamped on with an iron grip, and he dropped the Ovaro's reins and leaped. His other hand caught the tailgate as the Ovaro veered away. Fargo's booted feet bounced off the ground once before he was able to haul himself up and over the tailgate to go sprawling in the empty bed of the bouncing, jolting wagon.

He scrambled up to the front and climbed over onto the driver's box. The man who lay there was unconscious now but still bleeding from the gash on his head. Fargo thought the wound looked like someone had pistol-whipped the man. He caught hold of the man's clothes and hauled him up and over the back of the seat, dumping him into the wagon bed. Now that the man was in no danger of falling off, Fargo could turn his attention to the problem of stopping the team before the wagon reached the creek.

When he looked that direction, he saw that the stream was only a hundred yards away.

An expression of grim determination on his face, Fargo

**8**

took a deep breath, then dropped from the box into the singletree that ran between the four matched pairs of horses attached to the wagon. The singletree was narrow, but Fargo's sense of balance saved him, keeping him from plunging under the slashing hooves of the runaways. He put his left hand on the rump of one of the horses to steady himself, then bent his knees and reached down for the reins. They skittered and flopped just maddeningly out of his reach.

One foot slipped, and Fargo started to fall. He caught himself at the last instant, and at the same time, his fingers closed desperately around the reins. He straightened, hauled back on the reins, and called out to the horses. The team responded to the feel of a human touch on the harness and began to slow. Fargo brought the wagon to a halt less than ten yards from the creek.

His heart was pounding in his chest, and beads of sweat stood out on his forehead. He grinned, sleeved the sweat away, and stepped back up onto the box. As he settled down on the seat, a groan came from the man in the back. Fargo looked over his shoulder. The man lifted his head and shook it groggily. "Wh—what happened? Where are we?"

"Take it easy," Fargo told him. "Let's get this wagon back to town, and then we can figure out what happened."

He turned the wagon around, handling the team with ease now, and drove back into O'Bar. Fargo whistled for the Ovaro, who promptly made his way to the wagon and trotted along behind. Quite a few of the townspeople were standing in the street waiting for him, including Maddie Jenkins.

Fargo brought the wagon to a stop in front of the Red Top and dropped to the ground. "Somebody give this fella a hand," he said, gesturing toward the injured man who was trying to climb out of the wagon.

Fargo turned toward Maddie just in time to see her eyes widen. "Skye, look out!" she cried.

A hand came down hard on Fargo's shoulder and jerked him around. "You bastard!" somebody yelled, and a fist smashed into Fargo's face, knocking him back against one of the wagon wheels.

9

# 2

Fargo caught himself against the wheel. He tasted his own blood as his mouth began to swell up. He looked through narrowed eyes at the man who had struck him.

The dandy called Bart stood there, fists clenched, face mottled with fury. "That's twice you've stuck your nose in my business, you son of a bitch!" he raged. "I'm going to beat the hell out of you for that!"

Fargo straightened. Bart's two companions were still with him, and their hard, rugged faces showed that they would back their friend's play. No one was hurrying forward to side with Fargo, though. In fact, most of the townspeople were backing off, clearly afraid to get involved in this fracas.

Except for Maddie. She stepped forward, saying, "Get away from him! You don't have any right—"

"Shut up, whore," Bart said with a sneer as he shoved her back toward the saloon.

Slowly, Fargo lifted his left hand and wiped the back of it across his mouth. He glanced down at the crimson smear. That didn't bother him nearly as much as what Bart had just said and done to Maddie. A cold smile tugged at the corners of Fargo's mouth. "You said something earlier about teaching me a lesson," he said to Bart. "Well, come on, boy. I'm ready to go to school."

Bart grimaced, stepped toward Fargo, and swung a looping right hand at his head. One of the other men yelped, "Look out, Bart!" but it was too late. Fargo moved inside the punch, slipped it easily off his left shoulder, and buried his right fist to the wrist in Bart's belly. The blow had traveled only a short distance, but it packed most of Fargo's considerable strength behind it.

Bart's breath gusted out of his mouth and his face turned

pale as he bent over and staggered back. As he gasped for air, he flailed a hand at Fargo and managed to croak to his companions, "G-get him!"

The other two lunged at Fargo. The way they spread out and came at him from two directions at once told him they had more experience at brawling than Bart did. They would be more dangerous, too. Fargo had to take them seriously or he could wind up on the losing end of this fight.

He sidestepped quickly, bringing him closer to one of the men but farther away from the other. He had to take a punch, but he moved so that he was able to let it glance off the side of his head. The blow had plenty of power and still stung, but Fargo shook it off as he grabbed hold of the man's vest and swung him around into his partner. The men collided, their feet tangled, and both of them went down.

Fargo backed off, thinking it likely that both men wouldn't be able to get up at exactly the same time. That was how it worked out. One of the men rolled over and surged to his feet. Fargo was ready for him. He threw a right that rocked the man back on his heels, then clipped him with a left that sent him sprawling in the dust again. Fargo started to turn back toward the other man.

He had taken a little too much time with the first one, he discovered as the second man tackled him from behind. The man's weight landed solidly on Fargo's back, and his arm went around Fargo's throat and clamped down. It felt like an iron bar pressed across Fargo's windpipe, cutting off his air. He stumbled forward and fell to his knees.

Blood roared in his head. He drove his elbow up and back, smashing it into the midsection of the man who was choking him. The man's grip loosened slightly. Fargo hit him twice more, then bucked upward with his whole body. The man let go of him and fell off to the side.

Again the odds were against Fargo. He had disposed of one threat for the moment, but the other was waiting for him before he had time to react to it. The toe of a boot dug into his side in a vicious kick that sent him rolling over in the dusty street. As he came to a stop on his back, he saw the man rushing after him, foot upraised to stomp down into his face.

Fargo threw his hands up and caught hold of the boot as it started to descend. He heaved hard on it, and with a

*11*

startled yell, his opponent went over backward. Fargo rolled away to put some distance between himself and the two men, then came up onto hands and knees. Dust and sweat clogged his eyes and blurred his vision. He blinked them clear.

Bart's two friends were getting to their feet, looking a little winded and the worse for wear. The young dandy himself stood nearby watching the fight. Some of the color had come back into his face and he was no longer bent double, but he wasn't making any move to get back into the fight. Fargo supposed he was content to watch while his friends did his battling for him.

Fargo stood up, fists clenched, and waited for the two men to come to him. They approached even more warily now. He had more than held his own so far in this fight. Still, it was two against one, and they were confident that sooner or later they would vanquish him. He saw that in their eyes.

Some of the townspeople had left, but most of them were still standing around in a loose circle. Fargo's gaze flicked from person to person, saw that they were ashamed of themselves for not stepping in to put a stop to this, but at the same time, they were afraid. He didn't hold their inaction against them. They were just ordinary people, not gunmen or brawlers. They weren't the sort to go up against hardcases like the two he was facing now.

"Kill him!" Bart growled. "I want the bastard stomped into the ground!"

The other two were going to do their best to oblige.

Fargo knew he had to end this quickly. He couldn't just stand there all afternoon and continue to absorb punishment from two enemies. As the first man came within reach, he feinted with his left, and Fargo pretended to bite. He swayed, but instead of trying to block a punch that wouldn't come, he twisted around and put his back to the man, crouching slightly as he did so. The punch that the man actually threw sailed harmlessly over Fargo's shoulder. Fargo caught hold of the man's forearm, threw a hip into his body, and executed a neat toss that sent the man flying through the air to crash down senseless on his back.

Then he whirled around as the second man rushed in, and for a moment they stood toe to toe, trading punches, taking as much punishment as they handed out. Fargo was fighting on instinct now, and he realized that the man was using his right too much. He started slipping the blows on his left shoulder and moved inside to hammer the man's belly. That set him up for a left that rocked his head back and a sweeping right that caught him on the point of the chin. As Fargo stepped back, the man's eyes rolled up in their sockets and his knees buckled. He crumpled into the dirt.

It had been one hell of a fight, and Fargo knew he would be bruised and sore tomorrow, but right now the exultation of victory swept over him and a savage grin stretched his battered lips.

"Skye!" Maddie screamed behind him.

Fargo whipped around, still acting on instinct. His keen eyes spotted Bart standing by the wagon, the ivory-handled revolver grasped tightly in his hand. It had just cleared the holster and the barrel was beginning to tip up toward Fargo.

Time shattered into fractions of a heartbeat, as it sometimes did at moments like this. Fargo's hand darted toward the butt of the Colt on his hip. Bart's gun came level as Fargo's fingers closed around the Colt's smooth walnut grips. Smoke and flame blossomed from the muzzle of Bart's gun as Fargo drew. Fargo felt the wind of the bullet as it fanned past his face. Then his own revolver was out and rising into line, his thumb earing back the hammer as he lifted the gun. His finger closed on the trigger and the Colt bucked against his palm as it roared.

Bart slammed back against the wagon's sideboards, thrown into the vehicle by the bullet driving into his chest. He hung there for a second, eyes wide with pain and surprise, and then his gun slipped from his fingers to thud to the ground at his feet. A little blood seeped from the wound, reddening the area around the black-rimmed hole that Fargo's bullet had ripped in the white shirt. Bart fell to his knees, then pitched forward onto his face.

Fargo was reasonably certain Bart was dead, but he stepped forward anyway and kicked the fallen gun out of reach. Then he turned toward the other two men. They were still half stunned, but the earsplitting roar of gunshots had shocked some sense back into them. One of them said

**13**

to Fargo, "Don't shoot, mister. For God's sake, don't shoot!"

Fargo didn't have any intention of shooting anybody who wasn't trying to harm him or some innocent person. But he didn't holster his gun as he said to the two men, "Get up and get your friend's carcass out of here."

Shakily, the two men got to their feet and went over to Bart. One took his shoulders while the other grabbed his feet. They lifted the body and carried it down the street toward a barn, grunting with the effort required to do so. Fargo waited until they had taken Bart's corpse into the barn before he slid his Colt back in its holster.

"Skye, are you all right?" Maddie asked anxiously as she came up to him.

He nodded. "I reckon I am. Just a little bruised and scratched up. How's that fella who was on the wagon?"

"I don't know. A couple of men took him into the saloon."

Fargo took her arm. "Let's go see about him."

She hesitated. "Skye . . . you just killed a man."

"He didn't give me any choice in the matter," Fargo said flatly.

"I know that, but . . . still . . ." Maddie's voice trailed off, and she drew a deep breath. "You're right, of course. And I'm really glad it was him and not you who got carried off feet first."

"That makes two of us," Fargo said with a weary grin.

Most of the people had cleared off the street as soon as the shooting was over. Fargo and Maddie went into the Red Top and found the man from the wagon sitting at one of the tables, a wet cloth held to the gash on his head. He looked up as Fargo and Maddie approached.

"You must be the fella who stopped the wagon," the man said as he got to his feet. He stuck out a big, work-callused hand. "I'm Paul Washburn."

Fargo took Washburn's hand and returned the man's firm grip. "Skye Fargo."

"The one they call the Trailsman?" Washburn sounded surprised.

"Sometimes," Fargo admitted.

"Never expected to run into you, Mr. Fargo. I've heard plenty of yarns about you, though."

**14**

Fargo didn't point out that a lot of the stories Washburn might have heard about him were probably exaggerated. Instead, he asked, "How's the head?"

Washburn grunted. "Hurts like hell. But I reckon it'd likely hurt a lot worse if you hadn't stepped in to give me a hand."

"Sit down and tell me what happened," Fargo suggested.

Maddie said, "I think we could all use a drink," and went off toward the bar as Fargo and Washburn took their seats.

Washburn was a burly man in late middle age, with powerful shoulders and thickly muscled arms. His dark hair was lightly touched with gray. He said, "I was just drivin' my wagon into town when those three fellas jumped me. That little shit Bart had the other two hold me while he walloped me with his pistol. Just about knocked me out, but I had enough of my wits about me to know what they were doin'. They dumped me back on the seat and started yellin' and slappin' the horses with their hats. The team stampeded. I guess you know the rest. How'd you manage to get on the wagon and get them horses stopped, Mr. Fargo?"

"Just call me Fargo," the Trailsman suggested. "All I did was catch up to the wagon on my horse, jump on, and rein in the team."

"That's all, huh?" Washburn's expression made it clear that he considered it all a lot more complicated and dangerous than Fargo's simple explanation made it sound. "Well, I'm much obliged, Fargo. I reckon it would've been pretty bad if you hadn't done what you did."

"I'm just glad I was around to take a hand," Fargo said.

Maddie came back over to the table carrying a tray. "Our food and coffee got cold, Skye, so I brought us all some fresh coffee. I had Ted put some brandy in it, too."

That sounded good to Fargo. He took one of the cups from the tray Maddie placed on the table and sipped from it. Almost immediately, strength began to flow back into his body from the combination of coffee and brandy.

"Let me see that cut," Maddie went on. She fussed over the gash on Washburn's forehead for a few minutes, and the man's grin told Fargo that he was thoroughly enjoying the attention from the pretty, blond saloon owner. Finally, Maddie said, "I don't think you're going to need stitches, but you ought to have a doctor take a look at it to be sure."

"I'll do that when I get down to Fort Worth, ma'am," Washburn promised.

"You're on your way to Fort Worth, too?" Fargo said.

"Yep. Got to meet a fella there on business. I own a freight line, and I'm tryin' to get a contract with the army to run a route from Fort Worth out yonder to Fort Phantom Hill, in the Brazos River country." Washburn slurped down some coffee, then frowned. "I reckon that's why Bart and his pards jumped me. They were tryin' to keep me from gettin' to Fort Worth to meet up with that major fella."

Fargo didn't understand. "Why would they do that?"

"Bart's pa is Isaac Reese. Him and me, I guess you could say we're competitors. Me, I'd say Reese is a no-good son of a bitch who's been tryin' to put me out of business. Beggin' your pardon for the language, ma'am."

Maddie shook her head, clearly not disturbed by Washburn's description of Reese. "I didn't know Bart's last name or who he was, just that he and his friends have been hanging around here for the past few days."

"Waiting for me, more'n likely," Washburn said.

"Well, I'm still sorry he's dead, but—"

Washburn's coffee cup rattled on the table as he put it down. "Dead? Bart's dead?"

"He was trying to kill me after I beat his boys," Fargo said. "His shot missed. Mine didn't."

Washburn shook his head and groaned. "Damn, this ain't good. Reese sets a lot of store by that boy. When he hears that you killed Bart, he's liable to come after you. And he's still got two sons who're just about as rough as he is, not to mention half a dozen hardcases who work for him."

"It was a fair fight, and I didn't start it," Fargo said. "Reese'll just have to live with the outcome."

"Maybe," Washburn said, but he didn't sound convinced.

Maddie said, "I don't think you should try to go on to Fort Worth today, Mr. Washburn, not after being knocked out like you were."

Washburn thought it over, then shrugged. "I'm not supposed to meet Major Gilmore until tomorrow afternoon, so I reckon I could spend the night here and still get there in time. Is there a hotel in town?"

"No, but Mrs. Trask rents rooms in her house to travelers. I'm sure she could put you up for the night."

"I'm much obliged. Where'll I find this Mrs. Trask?"

"There are two rock houses on the western edge of town, back under some oaks. Mrs. Trask's is the second one."

Washburn drank the rest of his coffee, then got to his feet. "I'll mosey on down there."

Fargo got up, too, and retrieved his hat from the table where he'd left it before. "I'll go with you," he offered. "I was planning on moving on to Fort Worth myself, but after everything that's happened, I think I'll wait until tomorrow, too." He smiled at Maddie. "Thanks for everything, Mrs. Jenkins."

She bit her lower lip and nodded, looking like she wanted to say something. When she didn't, Fargo and Washburn went to the door of the Red Top and started to step outside.

"Skye, wait a minute!" Maddie called after them.

Washburn grinned at Fargo. "You best see what the lady wants. I'll go on. You can catch up to me."

Fargo thought about it, then nodded. "All right." It was possible that Bart's two cronies were still in town and might try to cause trouble for Washburn, but Fargo doubted it. They were probably fogging it back to Isaac Reese by now to tell him what had happened.

Maddie came out to join Fargo on the stone walk in front of the Red Top. "I'm glad you decided to spend the night here Skye," she said, "but you don't have to get a room down at Mrs. Trask's."

"Oh? Why not?" Fargo tried not to grin. He knew he shouldn't be teasing Maddie this way, but he couldn't help it.

"Because I have a perfectly good house with plenty of room down by the creek. Since your late lunch was ruined, I'd like to cook you a real supper, and then . . . well, we'll see what happens."

She looked up at him with warm brown eyes as she spoke, and suddenly Fargo no longer wanted to tease her. His face was serious as he said, "I'd like that, no matter what happens after supper."

She blushed, which just made her prettier, and said, "You'd better catch up to Mr. Washburn."

"Wait a minute. How do I find this house of yours?"

"What did he call you? The Trailsman? There's a trail out back here, behind the saloon. I think you can follow it."

Fargo chuckled and bent to brush his lips across hers. The quick kiss seemed to take her by surprise, but she didn't object. In fact, she looked rather pleased.

Washburn was dawdling along the street. Fargo's long strides enabled him to catch up, and when he did, Washburn said, "That's a mighty nice young lady."

"Yep," Fargo agreed. "She invited me to supper."

"You said yes, didn't you?"

"I did."

"Good," Washburn said. "I knew you were a smart young fella the minute I saw you." He sighed. " 'Course, that was before I knew you'd shot Bart Reese . . ."

---

# 3

Mrs. Trask was a widow who was more than happy to rent Washburn a room for the night. She exclaimed over the cut on the freighter's head just as Maddie had. Fargo figured he was leaving Washburn in capable hands, so he walked back down the street, got the Ovaro from the hitch rail in front of the saloon, and led the horse over to what appeared to be O'Bar's only livery stable. The hostler was impressed with the big black-and-white paint horse and promised to take good care of him.

Fargo paused in the street to take stock of things. He had some aches and pains from the tussle with Bart and the other two men, but overall he didn't feel too bad. And he had his evening with Maddie to look forward to, which lifted his spirits quite a bit. The only thing bothering him was that he had been forced to kill Bart Reese. He knew he wasn't going to lose much sleep over shooting a vicious bastard like Bart, but it was possible that Bart's death could lead to more trouble, more bloodshed. Fargo wasn't worried for himself, but when someone was out for revenge, sometimes innocent people got hurt.

All the more reason for him to move on to Fort Worth tomorrow. If Isaac Reese came looking for him, he wouldn't be in O'Bar anymore. Fargo considered forgetting about Maddie's invitation to supper and riding on tonight. If he didn't show up at her house, her feelings would be hurt, but better that than to have her get in the way of a stray bullet.

Then with a little shake of his head, he discarded the idea. Reese wasn't likely to show up looking for vengeance for a day or two, and by then Fargo would be long gone. The sun was already low on the western horizon. After being on the trail for a long time, he was going to take this night for himself.

The barbershop—like everything else, O'Bar had only one—was still open. Fargo dug out one of his few remaining two-bit pieces and paid for a bath. The barber groused a little about having to heat the water, but he did it. Fargo soaked for a while in a big wooden tub sealed with pitch, then dried off and pulled on a clean buckskin shirt from his saddlebags. The bath had made his sore muscles feel better, and his step was almost jaunty as he found the path behind the Red Top and started walking toward the creek in the dusk.

The ground dropped away fairly steeply behind the buildings on the west side of O'Bar's single street. The line of trees that marked the course of the creek ran north and south, paralleling the street, then curved to the east when it got south of town. Fargo realized it was the same creek where Washburn's wagon had almost crashed that afternoon.

The house at the end of the path under the trees was a sturdy log cabin, built in the Texas style with an open dog-trot in the middle. Maddie's husband must have built it for her before he brought her out from St. Louis, Fargo thought. He felt a twinge of sympathy for her. He hoped that she and her husband had at least had some good moments here before his untimely death.

One side of the cabin was dark, but lamplight glowed yellow through the oilcloth over the windows in the other side. Fargo went to that door and knocked softly, then took off his hat.

The door opened a moment later, and Maddie smiled out at him. "Good evening," she said. "I'm glad you came, Skye."

He took a deep breath, inhaling the delicious aromas that drifted out of the cabin. "So am I."

Maddie laughed and said, "Come on in."

She wore a plain blue dress tonight, instead of the more garish red gown she had sported in the saloon. Her fresh blond beauty made the outfit look elegant. The table had a cloth on it and was set with fine china. Maddie saw Fargo looking at it and said, "I hope this isn't too fancy for you, Skye. I . . . I don't get to entertain very often—"

"It's fine," Fargo told her. "In fact, it's lovely—just like you."

She laughed. "You don't know how good flattery sounds to a woman's ears when she lives in a place like this." She touched his arm, then drew her hand back as if unsure of herself. "Sit down, Skye. I'll get the food."

She had prepared fried chicken, potatoes, greens, and biscuits with honey. The food was even better than the meal he had started on in the Red Top that afternoon. Fargo hoped that nothing would happen to interfere with this one.

They talked as they ate, Fargo revealing little about his own background, as usual. But he learned how Maddie had grown up in St. Louis and met and fallen in love with a man named Harry Jenkins whose dream it was to go to Texas. Since she was in love with him, naturally Maddie had shared that dream. Harry had come out here first, gotten a start in business with the Red Top, and then sent for her.

"We had a few months together," she said as she set aside her fork. "Then . . ."

Fargo reached across the table and placed his hand on hers. "You don't have to go on," he said quietly. "The bartender in the Red Top told me what happened. I'm sorry, Maddie."

"I appreciate that. It's been a couple of years, but it still hurts sometimes."

"That's good," Fargo said. "That shows what you had was the genuine article, that it really meant something."

"Yes." She smiled and turned her hand over so that her fingers clenched his. "Yes, it did. Thank you, Skye."

They let a moment of silence stretch out between them. Before it could get uncomfortable, Fargo said, "I reckon I should go . . ."

"No." Maddie's hand tightened on his, and she leaned forward to look intently across the table at him. "Like I said, Skye, *it's been two years.*"

"You're sure that is what you want?" Fargo asked barely above a whisper.

She nodded. "I'm sure."

Fargo stood up, keeping hold of her hand, and Maddie came around the table and into his arms. She lifted her face to his. Fargo kissed her, relishing the warm sweetness of her mouth. As delicious as the food had been, Maddie tasted even better.

"Sweeter than honey," Fargo murmured.

"Oh," Maddie said. Her hands roved over him, touching him, exploring the hard muscles that she could feel through his clothes. While she was doing that, Fargo rained light kisses all over her face. She reached down to his groin with growing urgency and clasped her fingers over his hardness. "I can't wait any longer, Skye."

Neither could he. He blew out the lamp, then holding hands, they went across the dogtrot to the other side of the cabin. The silver moonlight that washed over the landscape was enough to guide their steps.

Once they were in the bedroom, Maddie lit a candle, then her fingers went to the buttons of her dress. "Let me," Fargo said. He unfastened the buttons with deft precision and spread the dress open, revealing firm, apple-sized breasts with brown nipples the size of half-dollars. Fargo bent his head to suck first one and then the other. Maddie's breasts rose and fell faster as Fargo's tongue licked around the erect buds. She ran her fingers through his thick black hair.

Fargo pushed the dress down around Maddie's hips and thighs and let it fall to the floor. She stepped out of it and kicked off the slippers she wore on her feet. She was completely nude. Fargo drew her into his arms and kissed her again, enjoying the sleek softness of her skin. He slid a hand down her back and explored the curves of her rump. "Skye . . ." she breathed against his mouth.

Her hands tugged at his buckskins. He unbuckled his gun belt and set it aside on a small table, then let Maddie peel his clothes off him. She gasped when his erect organ sprang free. "My God," she said as she wrapped both hands around it, and Fargo felt like saying the same thing as he felt her tantalizing caress. Instead, he gently urged her to the four-poster bed, which was covered with a thick, quilted comforter. She didn't pull the colorful comforter back but sprawled on top of it instead, sleekly beautiful in her nudity.

Fargo paused for a moment to drink in the sight of her, then slipped onto the bed with her. Her legs parted, revealing a triangle of fine blond hair that was a shade darker than what was on her head. In the candlelight, droplets of moisture glistened along the smooth pink furrow of her femininity.

Fargo's head dipped between her thighs. His tongue lapped along the folds of flesh, spreading them and opening her core to him. Maddie cried out sharply and her hips began to jerk. Long months of being without the touch of a lover had left her poised on the brink, and it took only a moment for her to plunge off into her climax. She bit down on a corner of the comforter to muffle her screams of ecstasy as Fargo drove his tongue in and out of her. Her hips bucked and her back arched off the bed.

When the exquisite spasms that shook her finally eased, she tried to catch her breath as she urged Fargo on top of her. "I'd like to return the favor," she said, "but right now I need you inside me!"

Fargo didn't mind postponing that particular pleasure until later. His shaft was throbbing with the need for release, and as he settled himself between Maddie's widespread thighs, she took hold of his manhood and guided him into her. A thrust of his hips sheathed him fully within her.

Her arms and legs locked around him as he began to pump in the ageless rhythm of man and woman. His climax built quickly, but he held off as long as possible to give her as much pleasure as possible. Finally, she began spasming again, and he took that opportunity to drive into her as deeply as he could. His own culmination shook him as he emptied himself inside her.

When it was finished, when they were sliding together down the long slope on the far side of the crest of their lovemaking, Fargo rolled onto his back and took her with him so that she was lying atop him with his shaft still lodged inside her. He stroked her hair as she breathed heavily against his chest. "Skye," she said between gasps, "that was so . . . so good . . . I had forgotten . . . thank you, Skye."

"No thanks necessary," Fargo told her. "I'm just glad I could be here for you tonight."

She lifted her head so that she could look at him. "You're staying the night, aren't you?"

Fargo chuckled. "I don't reckon you could get rid of me very easily now."

"Good," Maddie said as her hips started to move again, "because I'm just getting started. Why do you think I fed you so well? You're going to need your strength, Skye Fargo!"

Fargo lost track of how many times and how many ways they made love. When they both fell into a deep, dreamless sleep, it was well after midnight.

He woke up when the windows in the cabin were gray with the approach of dawn. Despite the fact that he had slept a relatively short time, Fargo felt refreshed and wide awake.

The fact that Maddie was leaning over his groin licking his erect manhood as she held it steady with one hand probably had something to do with how alert Fargo was. It would have been damned near impossible for any man's spirits not to perk up at that, he thought.

She took the head of the shaft into the warm, wet cavern of her mouth and began sucking. Fargo closed his eyes and spent several minutes reveling in the sheer pleasure Maddie was giving him. Then he reached over and ran his hand over her hip until he reached her thighs. His fingers stole between her legs and found her opening. She was already very wet, so he had no trouble slipping a finger inside her. A moment later he added another one.

After a few minutes, Fargo slid his fingers out of Maddie and took hold of her hips. He pulled her around so that she was straddling his head. She lowered her hips so that he could bring his mouth to her core. While he was positioning her, she continued her oral caresses, taking as much of his shaft into her mouth as she could and reaching between his legs to fondle him.

It wasn't long before both of them were ready to explode. Maddie swallowed greedily as Fargo's climax poured out of him. He kept his mouth clamped to her womanly furrow, drinking in the dew she gave him. Afterward, they both dozed off again, sleepily tangled in each other's arms and legs.

The next time Fargo awoke, it wasn't nearly as pleasant an experience. Someone was pounding on the door of the cabin.

He rolled out of bed and saw that it was a lot lighter outside now, indicating that the sun was up. He stepped over to the table where his gun belt lay and eased the Colt out of its holster.

On the bed, still snuggled in the comforter, Maddie shifted around and said, "Hmmm? Wha' . . ."

Fargo didn't know if she wanted anyone to know that he had spent the night with her, so he didn't call out to ask who was at the door. The knocking ceased for a moment, then resumed, and a mans' voice called, "Maddie? Mr. Fargo?"

Fargo recognized the voice. It belonged to Ted, the bartender from the Red Top. So, it was obvious Ted knew that Maddie had at least intended for Fargo to still be here in the cabin this morning.

Maddie sat up, shaking her head to clear away some of the night's cobwebs. She wrapped the comforter around herself and stood, then moved over to the door. "Ted?" she said through the panel. "What is it?"

Fargo laid the gun on the table and picked up his buckskin trousers. He slipped them on while Ted was saying, "Maddie, I thought you should know—Isaac Reese is in town."

Maddie gave Fargo a worried glance, then asked, "Are you sure?"

"I'm sure," Ted replied through the door. "I heard he

was down at Chambers's place a few minutes ago, talking about how he was going to even the score for Bart."

Fargo's jaw tightened. He hadn't expected Reese to show up in O'Bar quite this soon looking for vengeance. It was possible that Reese might blame Paul Washburn for Bart's death as well as Fargo. Someone had to warn Washburn that Reese was in town.

"Thanks, Ted," Maddie said. "You did the right thing to come and tell me."

"You'll tell Mr. Fargo?" Ted asked.

"I'll see that he knows about it."

The two of them stood there silently for a moment as they listened to Ted walk away, then Fargo said, "If you're embarrassed by this, Maddie, I'm sorry."

She pushed back her blond hair and shook her head. "I'm not embarrassed, Skye. I'm just mad that Isaac Reese had to show up so darned soon."

Fargo chuckled, but he was serious again a second later. As he continued pulling his clothes on, he asked, "Who's this Chambers that Ted mentioned?"

"He's a carpenter. He . . . makes caskets. I guess you could say he's the closest thing O'Bar has to an undertaker. That's where Bart Reese's friends took him yesterday."

Fargo grimaced. Maddie had given him pretty much the answer he expected. "Can I get to Mrs. Trask's place from here without going back up the main street?"

"Sure. Just follow the creek about a quarter of a mile, then turn east. That'll put you right in her backyard."

Fargo buckled on his gun belt, pulled on his boots, and picked up his hat. He turned to Maddie, who looked undeniably beautiful with the comforter wrapped around her and her smooth shoulders bare. He put his arms around her and bent his head to kiss her, and though their lips clung together for only a moment, the kiss was heated enough so that Fargo felt its power all the way down to his toes. "So long, Maddie," he said quietly. He turned toward the door and put on his hat.

She didn't call out to him as he left, and he was glad of that because it would have been difficult not to stop and answer. He had other things to concern himself with at the moment.

It was still early enough in the morning so that there was

a hint of coolness to the air in the shade of the trees along the creek. But it would be plenty hot before the day was over, Fargo knew. It always was in Texas in summer.

Despite the fact that he might be facing trouble, Fargo enjoyed the walk. Mockingbirds and bobwhites sang in the cottonwoods, and frogs splashed in the shallow creek. Squirrels leaped nimbly from branch to branch or scurried along the ground around the tree trunks. Sometimes one of them scolded Fargo as he strode along underneath them, a human interloper in a world they considered their own. At times of peace such as this, surrounded by nature, Fargo had a hard time believing there could be so much human misery in the world.

But then some son of a bitch always came along to remind him.

A few minutes later he was knocking at the back door of Mrs. Trask's house. The widow opened it, a look of surprise on her face as she saw Fargo. "Why, Mr. Fargo," she said. "What are you doing here?"

"Looking for Mr. Washburn," he said. "Is he still here?"

"Oh no." Mrs. Trask shook her head. "He left right after breakfast to go down and see about his wagon."

Fargo cast his mind back to the things he had seen the day before when he rode into O'Bar. The wagon yard was next to the livery stable, which meant it was across the street and a little to the north of the Red Top. And past the wagon yard was another small barn. That was where Bart's friends had carried his body. So that was where Isaac Reese was now, or had been recently, and to reach the wagon yard, Washburn would have had to walk right past . . .

No matter how he looked at it, this wasn't shaping up too good, Fargo thought. He tugged on the brim of his hat, said, "Much obliged, ma'am," to Mrs. Trask, and hurried around the house to the street. His long strides carried him quickly toward O'Bar's small business district.

He was half convinced that he would hear gunshots break out at any moment.

A buckboard rattled along the street, coming from the south, and Fargo saw a couple of riders. Other than that, O'Bar was its usual quiet self this morning. He came within sight of the barnlike shed where Chambers did his carpentry and built his caskets. Half a dozen horses stood quiet outside the place, and since there was no hitch rail, a man was waiting there holding the reins of all six animals. Fargo didn't recognize him, but he was the same sort of roughly dressed, hard-featured individual as the two men who had been with Bart the day before. To Fargo, that tagged him as one of Isaac Reese's men.

Fargo heard angry voices coming from somewhere behind the shed. As he approached, the man who was holding the horses glanced around and saw him coming. The hardcase dropped his free hand to the butt of the gun on his hip, but he was too slow. Fargo's Colt was already out of its holster and lined on the man's chest.

"Put those reins in your right hand and use your left to take out your gun," Fargo ordered. "Then drop it and kick it away."

The man followed Fargo's instructions, but then he surprised Fargo by shouting, "Isaac! Here's the other one!"

Fargo's mouth was a grim line. The hardcase had figured correctly that Fargo wouldn't gun him down in cold blood even if he called a warning to Reese.

That didn't stop Fargo from swinging a backhanded left to the man's mouth as he strode past. The man went down and let go of the gathered reins as he fell. The horses began to prance around nervously. The hardcase scrambled to his feet to try to catch them before they bolted. That would keep him busy for a few minutes, Fargo thought.

He stepped around the corner of the shed and saw Washburn, a man in a carpenter's apron who had to be Chambers, and five strangers. None of them had their guns drawn, and they were well aware that Fargo's Colt was already in his hand.

One of the men had Washburn backed up against the wall of the shed. He was a tall man in a black hat and dark brown duster. As he turned toward Fargo, the Trailsman saw that the man's face was craggy and tanned to the color of old saddle leather. Crisp white hair showed under the black hat.

"Are you all right, Paul?" Fargo asked Washburn. The burly freighter didn't show any signs of injury, but his face was flushed with anger.

"I'm fine, Fargo. Reese here was just wasting his breath threatenin' me."

"I wasn't making threats," Isaac Reese said in a cold, hard voice. "Just promises." He regarded Fargo with eyes like black stones. "You'd be the one they call the Trailsman." It was a statement, not a question. "The one who killed my boy."

"I'm sorry I had to do that," Fargo said honestly. "He threw lead at me first."

"Because you mixed in something that wasn't any of your business," Reese snapped. "I've heard all about it."

Fargo looked at the men with Reese and recognized the two he had fought with the day before. Their faces were bruised and puffy. The other two, Fargo had never seen before, but he could see the family resemblance between them and Reese. They would be the other two sons Washburn had mentioned.

"I didn't come here to get involved in any trouble between you and Washburn, Reese," Fargo said, "but I won't stand by while a man is killed. I won't take a beating without fighting back, either. I told you I'm sorry about what happened to Bart. The best thing for you to do now is move on, grieve your son, and stop trying to cause trouble for other people."

"Oh, I ain't even got started yet causing trouble," Reese said. "Washburn's going to be damned sorry he ever started down this way. I'll see to that. And as for you, mister . . ." An icy, humorless smile stretched across Reese's weathered face. "I'll see you in Hell." He gestured curtly to his companions. "Come on, boys."

They turned away from Washburn and strode toward the street. Reese's sons and the other two men all glared at Fargo as they passed him.

Fargo went to the corner of the shed and watched them mount up and ride away on the horses the first man had rounded up. They headed down the street, stopping alongside a freight wagon Fargo hadn't noticed before. It must have come up while he was behind the carpenter's shed, he thought. A slender young man sat on the driver's box, talking to Reese. After a moment, the driver flapped the reins and got his team moving. He drove the wagon out of O'Bar to the south. Reese and the others trotted their horses along beside it.

Washburn stepped up beside Fargo. "I'm obliged to you

again," he said. "When Malachi and Lucius grabbed me and dragged me back there, I thought I was a goner for sure."

"Are those Reese's other two sons?" Fargo asked.

Washburn nodded. "Yeah. Bart was the youngest boy. Those other two hardcases you tangled with yesterday are called Stilwell and Taylor. I don't know the fella who was holding the horses."

"They didn't hurt you?"

"Nope. Threw me up against the wall pretty hard, but that's all. Reese wanted to scare me, I reckon, maybe get me to beg for my life before they started whaling on me." Washburn grunted. "He'd've had a hell of a long wait for that."

Fargo grinned. "I believe it."

" 'Course, he's got just as big a grudge against you as he does against me. You'd better watch your back from here on out, Fargo."

"We'll watch each other's back," Fargo declared. He had reached a decision.

Washburn frowned in confusion. "What do you mean by that?"

"We're both headed for Fort Worth," Fargo said. "Seems like a good idea that we travel together for a while, just in case Reese tries to cause trouble."

"You'd throw in with me?"

"Seems like I already have." Fargo extended his hand. "Partners for now?"

"Sure." Washburn took Fargo's hand and pumped it. "A man would be a fool not to side with you, Fargo."

"We'll see about that. Like you said, I've got an even bigger target on my back."

Fargo was really more concerned with Washburn's welfare than his own, however. He had nothing tying him to this part of the country. He could turn and ride away and feel fairly confident that Reese would never catch up to him. Washburn, though, had to move on to Fort Worth and meet with that army major. Washburn's business was here in North Texas, and he couldn't just abandon it. Of the two of them, Washburn was more likely to face a threat from Reese. That had been true even before Fargo's deadly encounter with Bart. It seemed clear to him that Isaac

Reese would go to almost any lengths to prevent Washburn from getting that government contract. And Washburn was a freighter, not a gunfighter. Alone, he would be easy pickings for Reese and that gang of hardcases.

All those thoughts had flickered through Fargo's brain in a matter of seconds as he made up his mind to accompany Washburn to Fort Worth. Now Washburn said, "I'll see to my team and my wagon. I'll be ready to pull out in a half hour or so."

"Fine by me," Fargo said with a nod. That would give him time to say good-bye to Maddie.

# 4

The Ovaro rocked along at an easy pace as Fargo rode alongside Washburn's wagon. The trail rose and fell through the rolling, thickly timbered hills. Several times they had to ford creeks. Other streams had bridges built over them.

They talked as they traveled. Washburn telling Fargo about how he had been born and raised in an even smaller settlement to the north. "Had to work ever since I was just a sprout," the freighter said, "but I reckon I've made my way all right. Finally saved enough to buy a couple of wagons and started a freight line up at Preston, on the Red River. I put all the money I made back into the line. Now I've got plenty of wagons and routes running between Preston and Dallas, Jonesborough and Jefferson, over in East Texas. If I get this army contract to carry supplies to Fort Phantom Hill, it'll be the first time I've headed west. I figure it'll be a good foothold on the freighting business out there. Lots of folks are starting to move into the Brazos country."

"It could be pretty lucrative, all right," Fargo agreed. "What about Reese? Where's his business?"

Washburn snorted in disgust. "He's got a piddlin' little line that runs through some of the smaller settlements north of here like Alton and Pickneyville and Fitzhugh's Station, and over west toward Saint Jo, Montague, and Mesquiteville. He doesn't do half the business I do, but he don't seem to be hurtin' for money most of the time."

"Is that so?" Fargo murmured. The information didn't necessarily have to mean anything, but he filed it away in his brain anyway.

His thoughts drifted back to O'Bar—and Maddie Jenkins—for a few moments. His good-bye to her had certainly been bittersweet. They had kissed and held each other, and Maddie had whispered, "Next time you ride this way, Skye, you'd better stop and see me."

"I'll do that," he had promised. Maddie hadn't begged him to stay, or asked when he would be back, or any of the other things she might have done that would have just made the situation worse. What the two of them had together had been wonderful and special, and maybe someday it would happen for them again. But until that day came, they would move on with their lives, and if they looked back, it would be with fondness.

Fargo steered his attention back to the present. Even while he was thinking about Maddie, his senses had been alert. There was no telling when or if Isaac Reese would try to strike at them. They had to be ready for trouble.

There was no sign of Reese during their journey to Fort Worth, however. They had to cross three branches of the Trinity River before they reached the settlement in the early afternoon. The third branch of the river was at the very foot of the bluff on which Fort Worth sat. The wagon rattled across a bridge over the stream, then started up the steep trail that led to the top of the bluff. Fargo followed on the Ovaro.

His wanderings had brought him to Fort Worth before; he had been to most places on the frontier. He knew that a little over a decade earlier, the army had established a post here and named it after General Albert Jennings Worth. The stockade had sat atop this very bluff, which was high enough to provide a good view of the landscape to the west. At that time, there hadn't been much of anything out there except Comanches and Kiowas. Since the fort was established, all that had changed, and the growth of settlement toward the west was steady. The town that had grown up around the fort for which it was named was not large, but it was busy because it served as the jumping-off spot for much of that migration.

When they reached the top of the bluff, Washburn brought the wagon to a halt in front of a hotel. "This is where I'm supposed to meet Major Gilmore," he told Fargo. "I'll go in and see if he's here yet."

Fargo nodded and swung down off the Ovaro. He looked around the town as he looped the horse's reins over a hitch rail. Fort Worth had grown a little since the last time he was here, but he still recognized many of the businesses, including the saloon across the street called the Wild Jack. He recalled that the whiskey there had been at least decent on his last visit.

Leaning on the rail, Fargo looked up and down Fort Worth's main street. He didn't see the horses that Reese's bunch had been riding, nor did he spot the wagon that had left O'Bar with Reese. They had been traveling in this direction when they left O'Bar, but maybe they hadn't come to Fort Worth after all. Maybe Reese had decided to take Fargo's advice.

But Fargo didn't really believe that, not for a second. Every instinct he possessed told him that the trouble wasn't over.

Washburn came out onto the hotel's porch and said, "Major Gilmore's already here, Fargo. Come on inside."

"You go ahead and talk to him, Paul," Fargo told him. "This part of it is your business, not mine."

Washburn frowned. "I thought you said we were partners."

"Well . . . not business partners."

Washburn rubbed his jaw. "Then maybe I shouldn't have told the major that the Trailsman was going to help me lay out the route to Fort Phantom Hill if I get the contract."

Fargo felt a flash of irritation. Washburn had had no right to commit him to such an arrangement. On the other hand, Fargo was at loose ends right now and had said as much to Washburn during their trip down here. He had even said that he figured he would look for work when they got to Fort Worth. Clearly, Washburn had taken him at his word, and Fargo couldn't fault the freighter for that.

"I'll talk to the major," Fargo said as he stepped up onto the hotel porch, "but I can't promise anything beyond that, Paul."

Washburn put a hand on his shoulder and steered him into the building. "Thanks, Fargo. The major's waiting over here in the dining room . . ."

The tables in the dining room were covered with red-checkered cloths. The officer who stood up from one of them was medium height, with dark hair and a narrow mustache. He put out a hand and said, "Mr. Fargo? I'm Major Anthony Gilmore, United States Army."

Fargo shook hands with him. "Glad to meet you, Major."

Gilmore smiled. "Not as glad as I am to meet the famous Trailsman."

Fargo didn't say anything to that. He knew he had a reputation among military officers, frontier lawmen, and the like, but that was just a fact of life. He couldn't do anything about it one way or the other, so most of the time he just ignored it.

The three men sat down, and Gilmore went on, "Mr. Washburn tells me you've agreed to help him with the new route to Fort Phantom Hill, Mr. Fargo."

Before Fargo could say anything, Washburn spoke up. "I may have talked out of turn about that, Major. I can't make any promises for Fargo here. He may have other plans."

Gilmore's eyebrows went up. "Oh? Is that so?"

"Let's just wait and see how the conversation goes," Fargo suggested. "I haven't made up my mind what I'm going to do next."

"Well, if it means a better chance for a viable freight line between here and the fort," Gilmore said, "I hope you'll be part of the effort, Mr. Fargo."

"What has to be done in order to secure the contract?" Fargo asked.

"It's really quite simple—" Gilmore began, but then heavy footsteps from the hotel lobby interrupted him.

Fargo turned his head and saw a tall, powerful figure in a black hat and brown duster come through the arched entrance between the lobby and the dining room. So Isaac Reese had come to Fort Worth after all. Fargo wasn't a bit surprised.

Nor was he surprised that Reese's two surviving sons followed him into the dining room. Reese's third companion was a bit of a shock, though. Fargo recognized the slender figure as the driver of the wagon he had seen earlier in O'Bar.

What he hadn't been able to tell from a distance was that the driver wasn't a man at all but rather a young woman.

She wore a hat with a broad, floppy brim. Thick, light brown hair fell from under it and was pulled into a ponytail at the back of her neck. The denim trousers and man's shirt were a bit baggy, but not enough to completely conceal the lithe curves of her body. Blue eyes regarded Fargo coolly as she stood with her hands on her hips, just behind Reese and a step to his left.

"Major," Reese said, his voice rasping, "I suppose you know you're sitting with a couple of murderers."

"That's a damned lie!" Washburn burst out angrily as he started to get to his feet.

Fargo put out a hand to stop him. "Take it easy, Paul," he said.

Washburn settled back down in his chair, but only reluctantly. "Don't believe a word Reese says, Major," he muttered.

"What's this all about?" Gilmore asked.

Reese came closer to the table, trailed by his sons and the young woman. "That one there, the one called Fargo, killed my boy Bart up in O'Bar yesterday." He glared at Fargo, looking as grim as an Old Testament prophet.

"Bart drew and shot first," Fargo said. "I was just defending myself."

"So you admit that you killed Bart Reese?" Major Gilmore asked.

"I never denied it, and like I said, it was self-defense."

"And that was only after Bart and a couple of Reese's hired guns tried to kill me," Washburn put it.

Reese said, "Bart never tried to kill anybody. You picked a fight with him, then tripped and fell when you tried to get on your own wagon. It was your own fault your team stampeded."

"Again, that's a damned lie," Washburn insisted.

Reese's voice was like ice as he said, "I'm getting mighty tired of being called a liar."

The young woman said, "Pa, you know Bart could be a mite proddy—"

Reese turned on her, his hand coming up, and for a second Fargo thought he was going to slap her. Fargo's muscles tensed. He didn't want a fight here in the hotel dining room, but he couldn't just sit there while a woman was abused, even one who was evidently Reese's daughter.

Reese stopped the motion before he struck the young woman. As he lowered his hand, he growled, "Lucius, get your sister out of here. And Susannah, don't you ever let me hear you talk against family again."

She gave him a defiant look, but she didn't struggle as her brother Lucius took hold of her arm and led her out of the dining room. Reese swung back toward the table and went on, "If you want to do business with killers, Major, I reckon that's your business. I just thought better of the army, that's all."

Gilmore placed his hands flat on the table and said, "I'm not sure who to believe about this, but I know that it was decided Mr. Washburn was going to have first crack at that freight contract, Mr. Reese. You're interfering with government business, and I'll thank you to move on."

Reese didn't look happy about it, but he nodded. "Come on, Mal," he said to his other son as he turned toward the lobby.

The two of them stalked out. When they were gone, Major Gilmore said, "I don't like the sound of this, gentlemen. A heated business rivalry is one thing, but killings and beatings . . ." He shook his head.

"We told you the truth about what happened, Major," Fargo said. "Bart Reese would be alive today if he hadn't tried to ventilate me."

"Then I'd say the young man made a foolish choice indeed." Gilmore looked at Washburn. "As I was saying, the quartermaster has decided to put you to a simple test, Mr. Washburn. If you can take a wagon fully loaded with supplies from here to Fort Phantom Hill in a week's time, the contract is yours."

"A week!" Washburn exclaimed. "But it's close to a hundred and fifty miles between here and there!"

"A little more, actually," Gilmore said with a smile.

"We'd have to make over twenty miles a day," Fargo put in. "That's a mighty hard pace for a wagon."

"If you can't do it in that time, then we'll take note of how long it does take you," Gilmore said. "Mr. Reese will then be given a chance to beat that time."

"But if Fargo and me can do it in a week, then Reese is out in the cold?"

Gilmore shrugged. "Those are my orders. Make it in a week or less and the contract will be waiting for you at Fort Phantom Hill."

Washburn looked over at Fargo. "What do you think?"

Fargo turned over the proposition in his mind. On the face of it, the whole thing seemed impossible. A loaded wagon simply couldn't make the trip that fast.

But it was summer, which meant that the days were longer and there were more hours of light in which to travel. With enough moonlight and a good trail, it might even be possible to drive some at night. Finding the right trail would be up to him, Fargo thought. He would have to locate every shortcut he possibly could. And it would help if they had someone else to handle part of the driving, so that Washburn wouldn't become too exhausted to carry on. Given all that, it might be possible . . . just barely possible.

"We can't lose anything by giving it a try," he said.

"You're sure?" Washburn said.

Fargo nodded. "I think we can do it."

"Excellent," Gilmore said. He shook hands with both of them. "It's a deal, then. I'll be heading back to Fort Phantom Hill tomorrow. When can you get started?"

Washburn frowned in thought. "We'll have to pick up the supplies . . ."

"I took the liberty of leaving a list with the proprietor of the local emporium," Gilmore said. "You can pick up the load any time this afternoon, and at the very least, you'll be paid for delivering it to the fort, regardless of whether or not you're awarded the contract."

"Well, we'll get something out of the deal, then. We'll start first thing in the morning."

"Excellent." Gilmore came to his feet. "Good afternoon, gentlemen."

He nodded and left the dining room, passing through the hotel lobby to the street. Fargo looked at Washburn and suggested, "As long as we're here, we might as well get some lunch." He had just about enough money left to pay for his meal.

"Yeah, that's probably a good idea," Washburn agreed. "Maybe the last good surroundin' we get for a while."

So he was in the freight business now, Fargo thought later that afternoon as he loaded the last of the heavy cotton sacks of flour into the back of the wagon. He'd had worse jobs in his time, he supposed.

While they were eating lunch, he and Washburn had made it official, agreeing on a share of the freight charge that Fargo would receive in return for guiding the wagon to Fort Phantom Hill. If they made it there in a week or less and Washburn was awarded the government contract, Fargo would be paid a bonus.

But that was the end of it. Fargo made that clear. Win or lose, he was only going to make the one trip to the fort. Washburn wouldn't need him after that, and he was going to drift on, giving in to his restless nature.

Washburn stepped back and regarded the fully loaded wagon parked in front of the emporium. He said, "I'd sure hate for anything to happen to these goods. Reckon I'd better spend the night standing guard over them."

"Maybe we can hire somebody to do that," Fargo said. "We need to see if we can find somebody to come with us and handle some of the driving chores, too. Maybe the same person might take both jobs."

Washburn thought about it and nodded. "That's not a bad idea. Where'll we find somebody, though?"

"Maybe the fella who owns this store might know someone," Fargo said, nodding toward the aproned storekeeper who stood on the establishment's loading dock.

When Fargo and Washburn had explained their problem, the storekeeper pondered for a moment, then said, "So you need somebody who can handle a team as well as guard that cargo? I know just the hombre. Name's Sparks. He's an old stagecoach jehu, but he's done some shotgun guardin', too."

"Sounds perfect," Fargo said. "Where do we find him?"

"You might try over at the newspaper office. The last I heard, he was trying to fix a broke-down printing press for them. He likes to tinker with things, claims he can fix just about anything mechanical."

Fargo and Washburn walked down the street to the offices of the Fort Worth *Star*. When they asked for Sparks, a slick-haired editor with a string tie and sleeve garters sent them into a large back room full of ink-smeared metal parts. A skinny old man knelt in the middle of the chaos. He was as ink-smeared as the printing press, which evidently he had taken apart. He was staring at a piece of the apparatus in his hand. He didn't look up as Fargo and Washburn entered the room.

"Are you Mr. Sparks?" Washburn asked.

"Eh?" The old man finally noticed them. He held out the part in his hand and asked, "You wouldn't happen to know where this goes, would you?"

"I don't have the foggiest notion," Washburn replied.

"I've taken this blasted thing apart and put it back together half a dozen times, but I've always got this piece left over." The old man shook his head. "Oh well, I don't reckon it really needs to be in there anyway." He set the piece of metal aside and stood up. He wiped his hand on his overalls and extended it. "I'm Sparks. No 'mister,' just 'Sparks.'"

Fargo and Washburn shook hands with him and introduced themselves. "We're on our way to Fort Phantom Hill with a wagonload of supplies," Washburn said. "The gent over at the general store said you might be willing to hire on to go with us. We need an extra driver and somebody to guard the supplies tonight."

Sparks stuck both hands in his pockets and started jingling some coins he had there. "Reckon I could do that. What's the job pay?"

Washburn hesitated, then said, "I could go ten dollars, I suppose."

Sparks nodded. "That'll do. Where'd you leave this here wagon?"

"Over at the store."

"You'll want to move it. That's not a good place to leave a wagon parked. How you gettin' to Phantom Hill? Which trail you takin'? Where you plan to stop over?"

This old-timer was full of questions, Fargo thought, looking down at the floor to conceal a grin.

"We'll just have to deal with all that as we come to it," Washburn said, holding up his hands to stop the flow of questions from Sparks.

Fargo asked a question of his own. "Do you have a gun?"

"Scattergun," Sparks said with a nod. "And I know how to use it, too. Drove and guarded for John Butterfield up in Missouri and Ben Holladay out in California. I'd probably still be workin' for Butterfield if his health hadn't gotten bad and that fella Dinsmore tooken over the company. Dismore and me never did get along. I figured I'd get me a run on that new overland route, but Dinsmore said I was too old." Sparks snorted. "Too old! Well, come on, I'll get my greener and then we'll go move that wagon."

Fargo indicated the torn-apart printing press. "What about all this?" he asked curiously.

"They got another one," Sparks said. "I'll get back on it later, after I do that job for you boys. Wish I could get some sort of drawin' of the thing that shows how it's supposed to go together . . ."

As the three of them left the newspaper office, Fargo made a mental vow never to let Sparks take anything apart.

One thing Fargo had noted about Washburn was the freighter's prodigious appetite. Washburn would pile up a plate with food, then go back for seconds and even thirds after finishing it off. Sparks, however, ran Washburn a close second in the eating department, but he was rail-thin while Washburn was rather beefy. The two men seemed to get along well, which was the important thing, considering that they would be working closely together over the next week as they tried to get the wagon to Fort Phantom Hill in time for Washburn to win that government contract.

Fargo was tapped out. Washburn paid for supper for all three of them and rented hotel rooms for himself and Fargo, as well as putting up the Ovaro in the livery stable along with the wagon team. Sparks was going to sleep under the wagon with his shotgun. Fargo would have enjoyed paying a visit to the Wild Jack for a few shots of whiskey and maybe a hand or two of poker, but he wasn't going to let Washburn pay for that, too. Besides, they intended to get an early start in the morning, so it wouldn't hurt to turn in and get a good night's sleep, Fargo told himself.

He had taken off his boots and shirt, leaving him stripped to the waist. His hat, his gunbelt, and the Arkansas toothpick that he usually carried in his boot lay on the small table that was the room's only piece of furniture other than the bed and a straight-backed chair. His Henry rifle was leaning in a corner. He was about to peel off the buckskin trousers when a knock sounded on the door.

Fargo slipped the Colt from its holster and went to the door. He took a quick step to the side even as he called, "Who is it?" Too many careless people had been killed when somebody shot through a hotel room door. Careless was just about the last word anybody would use in describing Skye Fargo.

The person on the other side of the door didn't answer Fargo's question. Instead, a woman's voice asked, "Mr. Fargo?"

The voice was a little familiar, but Fargo couldn't place it immediately. With the Colt held ready in his hand, he reached over, turned the knob, and flung the door open. The woman standing there in the hotel corridor gave a gasp of surprise at the suddenness of the door's opening.

Susannah Reese looked at Fargo's bare chest and the gun in his hand and asked coolly, "Is that the way you always greet visitors, Mr. Fargo?"

# 5

Fargo looked past Susannah, checking the hallway for any sign of her father or brothers. When he didn't see them, he lowered the Colt to his side but kept his thumb on the hammer, ready to cock it if need be. "What are you doing here, Miss Reese?" he asked.

"Aren't you going to invite me in?" Susannah said in return.

"I always try to be polite to ladies, but I think I'd like to have some idea what you want before I let you in."

She sighed. "I just want to talk to you, Mr. Fargo. That's all."

Fargo considered for a second, then nodded. He stepped back and motioned for Susannah to come in. She did so, closing the door behind her. Fargo lifted an eyebrow quizzically at that gesture.

"My father doesn't know I'm here," Susannah said by way of explanation. "I don't want anybody coming by in the hall and seeing me. They might tell him where I am."

Fargo went to the table and slid the gun back in its holster. He reached for the shirt he had draped over the back of the chair and said, "Let me get dressed . . ."

"You don't have to bother on my account," Susannah said. "I have—had—three brothers. I've seen all there is to see."

"I'm not your brother," Fargo said. Susannah's reminder that only a day earlier he had killed one of her brothers made him a bit uncomfortable. He slipped the shirt over his head.

Susannah took off her hat and tossed it on the bed without asking permission. She undid the ribbon around the ponytail and shook out her long light brown hair, running

**41**

her fingers through it. She was a very attractive young woman, Fargo noted, despite the man's clothes she wore.

"Mr. Fargo, I'll speak plainly."

"Good," he said.

"I don't hold it against you that you shot my brother. Bart was a mean son of a bitch. I grew up with him, so I know that just about as well as anybody." She paused and shook her head. "I'm not saying that I didn't grieve for him when I heard that he was dead. I did. At times like that, people usually remember the good times they've had with a person, even if there weren't very many, and forget about the bad. But I know he brought it on himself."

"I didn't ride in there looking for trouble," Fargo said. "I didn't even know your brother."

"It didn't take long for people to get to know Bart, and when they did, they usually didn't like him. Like I said, he had a mean streak. Still, he was family, and that's why I'm here."

Fargo tensed slightly. Was she looking for vengeance, despite what she'd said about not blaming him for Bart's death?

"How do you mean that?"

"You've got to stick up for your family, no matter how rotten they are. So I've come to ask you not to throw in with Paul Washburn."

That surprised Fargo a little. "I've already agreed to go along with him."

"Then back out," Susannah pleaded. "I've heard of you. We all have. It's going to be mighty hard for Washburn to make it to Fort Phantom Hill in a week, but with the Trailsman helping him, he might have a chance. Without you, he'll never make it, Mr. Fargo."

"You think your father would get the government contract if Washburn fails." It was a statement, not a question.

"I know he will. We need that contract, Mr. Fargo."

Fargo ran a thumbnail along his bearded jaw. "I've heard that your father's freight line makes good money, even though he doesn't haul as much as Washburn does."

"It may seem like it, but that's not the case," Susannah said with a shake of her head. "Without that army contract, the line may go under."

Fargo didn't know whether to believe her or not. Isaac

Reese didn't act like a man whose company was on the verge of failure. Maybe his arrogance, though, was just a cover-up for his problems.

It didn't really matter. Fargo said, "I've given my word to Washburn. I'm not going back on it."

Susannah came a step closer. "Are you sure? It would really help us out. I'd be more grateful than I can say, Mr. Fargo. Me personally, I mean."

Fargo's eyes narrowed. "Did your father send you here?"

"No! I told you, I don't want him to know I'm here."

"I know what you told me," Fargo said.

"So you're calling me a liar?" Susannah's blue eyes flashed fire.

"I'm just not sure what to believe."

"Believe this," Susannah said. "I don't want you to help Washburn, and I'm willing to do whatever it takes to see that you go along with me." She held up a hand to stop him as Fargo opened his mouth to speak. "I know, you gave your word. And I'm sure that's important to you. But is it important enough to make you turn down what I'm offering?"

"And what exactly is that?" Fargo asked coolly.

Susannah's lips tightened, and the area around her mouth paled with strain. "You're going to make me spell it out, aren't you?"

Fargo nodded. "I'm afraid so."

She looked at him for a moment longer, then said, "All right." Her hands came up to the buttons of her shirt and began unfastening them.

Fargo watched, his face carefully expressionless, as Susannah unbuttoned the shirt and spread it open to reveal high, firm breasts. The nipples were pale pink and soft at the moment, but as Fargo studied them, the little buds of flesh began to harden. Susannah's chest and throat and face reddened with embarrassment or excitement, or maybe some of both. She cupped her breasts in her hands and said, "You can do whatever you want with me, Fargo."

"In return for going back on my deal with Washburn?" Fargo shook his head. "I can't do that."

"Damn it!" Susannah burst out. "Don't you want me? Aren't I pretty enough for you?"

"You're a lovely young woman," Fargo said honestly,

"and under other circumstances I'd have you on that bed right now, but you can't bribe me this way, Susannah. Or any other way, for that matter."

"You son of a bitch!" she hissed. Her breasts rose and fell more quickly now as anger mixed with passion. "You mean I got myself all worked up to come over here—"

"That was your choice," Fargo drawled.

"And then you just . . . just . . . turn me down . . . Oh!" Her hand lashed out toward Fargo's face.

He caught her wrist before she could slap him. She tried to knee him in the groin, but he turned and took the blow on his hip. As her other hand shot toward his face, fingers hooked into claws and aimed at his eyes, he caught that wrist, too, and swung her around. A shove sent her sprawling on the bed.

"You bastard!" she cried as she bounced up. "You can't do this!"

"I won't abandon Washburn," Fargo said.

"To hell with that stupid contract! I don't care about that anymore." She came toward him, but she was no longer attacking him. "I don't care about any of it except you, Fargo."

This time when she reached for him it was out of need, not anger. Her arms went around his neck and drew his head down to hers. Her lips found his mouth. She crushed herself against him, molding her body to his so that her breasts were flattened against his chest.

Fargo was still wary, but his own excitement was growing to the point that it wouldn't be denied. If Susannah didn't get out of here now, there would be no turning back.

He broke the hot, passionate kiss. Susannah moaned, "Fargo . . ."

"I won't break my word," he said one last time.

"I don't care about that. Just take me. Make love to me."

Well, since she put it that way, Fargo thought, he could probably oblige her.

They moved together toward the bed, kissing again. Fargo slid the shirt off Susannah's shoulders and dropped it on the floor. She took her mouth away from his long enough to catch hold of the bottom of his shirt and pull it up and over his head. She tossed the garment aside and then rested her hands on his chest. Leaning down, she licked one of his nipples. As she straightened, she tossed her head to throw her hair back and smiled at him.

Fargo cupped her breasts, gently squeezing the soft, creamy flesh. Her nipples were fully erect now. He strummed them with his thumbs. Susannah's eyes grew heavy-lidded, and she sighed.

Fargo unfastened her jeans and slid them down over her hips, taking her underwear with them. He paused, kneeling before her, and rested his face against the soft, fur-covered mound at the juncture of her thighs. She put her hands on his head and pressed him harder against her.

Putting his left arm around her knees, Fargo placed his right hand on her belly. A simple push dropped her back onto the bed. He came to his feet and pulled her boots and socks from her feet, followed them with the trousers that were bunched around her ankles. With her legs in the air like that, he had a good view of her sex, the wet pink slit surrounded by downy brown curls.

He stepped back and took off his own trousers. As he came back to the edge of the bed, Susannah sat up and reached for him. Her hands went around his long, thick shaft. She leaned forward and took him in her mouth, sucking tenderly but insistently. The tip of her tongue toyed with the underside of his maleness, lingering around the crown.

Fargo enjoyed the sheer heat of her mouth on him, but after a few moments he tangled his fingers in her long brown hair and moved her head away from his groin. He leaned down to kiss her again, and as he did so, she slowly reclined on the bed. Fargo went with her, lying atop her. His hips sank into the soft cradle of her spread thighs. She didn't have to guide him home. His hardness centered in on her portal. A tiny shudder went through her as the tip of his shaft touched her opening. She put her arms around his neck and kissed him harder as her hips thrust up. Fargo thrust at the same time, and in one hot, blinding instant, he was fully inside her.

Her feminine muscles clamped down hard on his throbbing manhood. Her mouth opened wide as Fargo's tongue slid between her lips. Her tongue met his, and they circled each other wetly in a dance of passion.

Fargo's hips pumped in a steady rhythm, pistoning his

shaft in and out of her. Susannah met him thrust for thrust and began to pant into his mouth as her excitement rose. She tore her lips away from his and tossed her head from side to side, caught in the grip of a passion that would not be denied. For long minutes he stroked her higher and higher toward the crest.

At last she cried out and began to buck frenziedly beneath him. Only then did Fargo let himself go. His hips were almost a blur as he drove in and out of her and she spasmed around him. When he couldn't hold off anymore—when he didn't want to hold off anymore—he froze with his organ buried as deeply inside her as it would go.

They peaked together, then began the long, dizzying fall together. When Fargo tried to roll off her, Susannah's arms tightened and held him there as she seemed to relish his weight and the feel of his shaft slowly growing soft inside her. Fargo kissed her, and she smiled sleepily up at him and whispered, "Can I stay . . . just for a little while?"

"Stay as long as you want," Fargo said.

After blowing out the lamp, he dozed in the darkened room with Susannah snuggled up against him, but he didn't fall completely asleep. They were spooning, with her back against his front, his still partially-erect shaft resting intimately in the cleft of her buttocks. Fargo's breathing became deep and regular, as if he were sound asleep, but a tiny part of his brain was still alert and aware of what was going on in the room.

So he knew it when Susannah slid away from him and slipped out of the bed, and alarm bells began to jangle in his mind. Even though his breathing wasn't disturbed, he was fully awake by the time she reached the door of the hotel room and quietly opened it.

The light that spilled into the room from the corridor was very faint. They must have blown out the lamp farther down the hall, Fargo thought as he saw the two dark, bulky shapes loom out of the shadows. His eyes were keen enough so that even in the darkness he could see that each man was holding something. They lifted the objects as they approached the bed where they thought he was sleeping.

Fargo was filled with anger—anger that the Reese brothers would try to kill or injure him, anger that Susannah would seduce him and then try to betray him. He was certain these two shadowy nocturnal visitors were Lucius and Malachi Reese. They drew closer to the bed, the bludgeons in their hands poised to strike.

Maybe they just planned to break his arms and legs, Fargo thought. But that was bad enough. Whatever happened now, they had brought it on themselves.

Because it was a warm night, and because Fargo still hadn't fully trusted Susannah, they had been lying on top of the sheets, rather than underneath them. So there was nothing to tangle around Fargo and slow him down as his magnificently honed reflexes sent him rolling off the bed even as the clubs in the hands of the Reese brothers swept down. Fargo landed on his feet, hearing the dull thuds as the clubs smacked into the mattress where he had been lying an instant earlier. The two men were leaning forward as their murderous blows landed. Fargo raised his right leg and kicked the closest one in the head.

Fighting naked and unarmed wasn't his idea of a good time. The worst part of it was that all his weapons were on the other side of the bed, the side where the Reeses were. He had to have a weapon of some kind if he hoped to survive this battle.

As the man he had kicked fell over backward, the other one leaped onto the bed and slashed at Fargo's head with the club. Fargo ducked under the wild swing, hearing the club swish through the air above him. The man lost his balance as the mattress gave under him, and he toppled forward toward Fargo. Fargo's hand closed over the back of the room's single chair and whirled it around. The man grunted in pain and his breath puffed out of him as one of the chair legs jabbed him in the belly. Fargo let go of the chair and darted aside, letting the man fall onto the chair and smash it into kindling.

Fargo heard the rush of footsteps and bent down to feel around on the floor. One of the broken chair legs had slid over beside him. He found it after a couple of seconds and snatched it up. As he straightened he whipped the chair leg around. The other man's club brushed Fargo's left shoulder, but he felt a satisfying impact as the chair leg thudded into something solid.

Sliding to the side, Fargo jabbed with the chair leg, then

slashed it from side to side, protecting himself as he got his back to a wall. Now they could only come at him from one direction. He was still at a disadvantage, though, outnumbered two to one and armed with only a broken chair leg.

So far the battle had been fought in near silence, with only a few thuds and grunts to indicate that a deadly struggle was going on. Fargo wondered fleetingly what had happened to Susannah. Had she fled after letting her brothers into the room? Or was she still here, waiting to see what was going to happen?

He wouldn't put it past her to get in on the fight herself, he decided.

The Reese brothers were big and slow and would never be able to move as silently as the man called the Trailsman. Fargo heard them coming as they charged him. He ducked, thrust out the chair leg, and again felt it strike something. A man yelped in pain. Fargo hoped it had gotten him in the groin. That was about the level at which he'd been aiming.

A club hit him on the left thigh, sending pain shooting down his leg. Fargo gritted his teeth and swung the chair leg. It clashed with something, fending off another blow of the club. But the impact loosed Fargo's grip on the chair leg, and it slipped out of his hand.

He threw himself forward in a rolling dive, slamming into someone's knees. Fargo grabbed hold of the legs and heaved. His opponent crashed to the floor beside him. Fargo came up on his knees, stuck out his left hand, and felt it brush against a man's chest. That allowed Fargo to aim his right fist at the spot where the man's jaw should be. The punch was right on the money, crashing into the man's face and driving him back down to the floor.

An arm looped around Fargo's neck from behind, surprising him and cutting off his air. He drove an elbow back into his attacker's midsection. That loosened the grip for a second, just long enough for Fargo to gulp down a breath. He used his elbow again, then reached back with his left hand and got hold of an ear. A savage twist made the man yell right in Fargo's ear. When Fargo hit the man in the belly a third time with his elbow, the man let go and rolled away.

Fargo pounced like a giant cat, landing with his knees on the man's belly. He grabbed hold of the man's neck and bounced his head off the floor a couple of times. The man went limp underneath him.

Fargo stood up. It had been a desperate battle, fought mostly in the dark, and his chest was heaving from the exertions he'd been forced to endure in order to save his life. His left leg ached from the blow on his hip. He was all right, though, clearheaded and ready for more trouble if it came.

He stepped over to the small table beside the bed, felt around on it for the matches he'd left beside the lamp. Finding one, he snapped it into life with his thumbnail and held the flame to the wick of the lamp. Fargo narrowed his eyes against the glare as the wick caught and a yellow glow welled up to fill the room.

Surely someone had heard the commotion in here, and it was possible the law had been summoned. Fargo didn't want the sheriff showing up and finding him naked. He turned around to look for his pants, and as he did so, he saw exactly what he expected to see: Lucius and Malachi Reese stretched out on the floor, both of them out cold.

But where was Susannah?

Fargo's back was to the open door. When he heard a whisper of sound, he glanced over his shoulder to see Susannah lunge out from behind the door, still nude, his own Arkansas toothpick gripped in her hand as she tried to plunge it into his back. Fargo whirled around and got his left hand up in time to grab Susannah's wrist and twist the knife aside. As he hauled her past him, his right fist came up and clipped her slightly on the chin. The blow sent her sprawling on the bed. The knife clattered on the floor where she dropped it.

While Susannah was stunned, Fargo grabbed his buckskin trousers and tugged them on. By the time Susannah recovered her wits and sat up on the bed, blinking rapidly and glaring at him, he had his Colt in his hand.

"Get your clothes on and get the hell out of here," he said coldly.

"You bastard! After what you did—"

"I did what you asked me to do," Fargo broke in. A groan came from one of the men on the floor. Fargo went on, "I'll tell you again. Get dressed and get out. And take your brothers with you."

"You'll be sorry about this, Fargo."

"I already am." Though he didn't want to prolong this, curiosity prompted him to ask, "What was the plan? If you could get me to go along with what you wanted using your fair white body that would have been the end of it? But if I was stubborn, you'd take me to bed and then let your brothers into the room while I wasn't expecting an attack? That's the way the hand played out."

"Think whatever you want," she snapped as she angrily jerked her shirt on. "And go to blazes while you're doing it!"

Fargo stepped back, both to give her some room as she got dressed and so that he could keep an eye on her brothers, both of whom were now showing sign of regaining consciousness. One of them managed to sit up. He held his head in both hands and groaned. After a moment, he looked up at Fargo, and his lips drew back from his teeth in a grimace of hate.

"Come on," Susannah said. "Get Mal on his feet and let's get out of here." She hadn't buttoned her shirt, and it still hung open. If she cared that her bare breasts were exposed to her brothers, she gave no sign of it.

Lucius Reese hung on to the bedstead and pulled himself to his feet. He reached down and slapped his brother Malachi a couple of times. "Wake up, you stupid bastard," he said. Malachi came to his senses, and Lucius helped him stand up shakily.

Susannah jammed her hat on her head and finally got around to buttoning her shirt and tucking it into her denim trousers. She took one of Malachi's arms and helped Lucius get him to the door. As the two brothers stumbled out into the hotel corridor, Susannah paused and looked back at Fargo.

"If you go through with helping Washburn, Fargo, there's no telling what'll happen to you. But it won't be pleasant. You can consider that your last warning."

"I can't be scared off any more than I can be bought off," Fargo returned coolly. "Tell your father he'd better be careful that what he does doesn't come back to haunt him."

Susannah didn't say anything to that. She just glared at Fargo and then moved off down the hallway after her brothers, heading toward the stairs. Fargo stepped out, glanced along the corridor, and saw several curious faces peering at him from half-open doors. He smiled and said, "No trouble, folks. Just a little misunderstanding."

The words probably would have sounded more convincing, he realized, if he hadn't been standing there half naked with a gun in his hand.

<hr />

# 6

Despite the fact that he hadn't gotten a full night's sleep, Fargo was awake before dawn the next morning. He splashed water from the basin on the table in the hotel room on his face, then got dressed and went down to the dining room. Several early risers were already there, including Paul Washburn The freighter had two empty plates shoved aside on the table and was working on a third piled high with food. He saw Fargo and lifted a hand in greeting. The hand had a biscuit in it.

Fargo went across the room, pulled out a chair, and sat down at the table with Washburn. "Looks like you're movin' a mite stiff this morning," Washburn commented.

"I'm fine," Fargo said. He was confident the soreness would be gone from his leg in a day or two. As it was, he knew he could ride without any trouble.

A plump waitress with a friendly smile came over and took Fargo's order for bacon, flapjacks, and coffee. While Fargo was waiting for his food, Washburn finished off his breakfast, drained the last of the coffee from his cup, and said, "I'll go spell Sparks so he can get some grub, then I reckon we'll be ready to go."

Fargo nodded. "Keep your eyes open," he said. "I don't trust those Reeses." He didn't mention the attempt on his life that Lucius and Malachi had made the night before, nor Susannah's part in it. Washburn knew to be careful without Fargo having to go into that.

"I don't trust 'em, neither," Washburn said. He stood up, put his hat on, and ambled out of the dining room.

Fargo's food had just arrived at the table when he heard an angry shout from the street. Recognizing Washburn's voice, he bolted to his feet and ran out of the hotel, the thought flickering through his head that it seemed like he hardly ever got to eat a meal in peace these days.

A flicker of flame in the predawn gloom caught Fargo's eyes as he emerged on the hotel porch. The light came from down the street, toward the general store. They had parked the loaded freight wagon in the alley next to the emporium for the night. Fargo's heart thudded in his chest as he broke into a run in that direction.

His suspicions were confirmed as he came to the mouth of the alley and saw flames licking up one side of the canvas covering over the back of the wagon. Washburn was trying to beat out the fire with a burlap bag of some sort. A dark shape lying on the ground nearby was probably Sparks, but Fargo couldn't be sure of that. There was no time now to check, either.

Fargo glanced around. Rain barrels stood at various spots along the street. One of them was at the other corner of the emporium. Fargo dashed over to it, snatched up the bucket that sat beside the barrel, and filled it. He ran back to the wagon and flung the water on the flames. That helped, but it wasn't enough to put out the fire.

Feet pounded up behind Fargo. Thinking this might be a new threat, he whipped around, his right hand dropping to the butt of the Colt. Instead of an enemy, he saw the face of one of the townspeople. The man's features were given a garish cast by the flickering light of the fire.

Fargo thrust the bucket in the man's hand. "Bucket brigade!" he snapped.

The man turned and ran off, bound for the rain barrel. More citizens showed up in the mouth of the alley. Shouts of "Fire! Fire!" went up and down the street.

Frontier communities like Fort Worth lived in mortal fear of an out-of-control conflagration. A fire could spread from building to building in a matter of moments, and if it wasn't contained in the early stages, a blaze could quite easily wind up burning down an entire town. Most people kept a bucket of water handy, just in case.

Within minutes, the bucket brigade had formed a line

between the rain barrel and the burning wagon on the other side of the building. Fargo took the buckets as they were handed to him, water sloshing over their tops, and threw the water on the flames. Washburn stomped out sparks that flew from the wagon and used the burlap bag to quickly beat out any small fires that started up in the alley. The fire had only really gotten started on one side of the wagon's canvas cover, so it didn't take long to extinguish the blaze.

When the fire was out, Fargo stepped back, an empty bucket dangling from his left hand, a grim expression on his face. There was no doubt in his mind what had happened here. He dropped the bucket and turned to the sprawled figure on the ground he had spotted earlier.

Fargo knelt beside the man and rolled him over. It was Sparks, all right. A groan came from the old man, and Fargo felt a surge of relief that Sparks was still alive, at least.

Sparks lifted a hand to his head and tried to sit up. "Wha . . . what happened?"

Fargo put an arm around the old man's skinny shoulders and propped him up. "You tell us," he said. "The wagon was on fire when we got here."

"Somebody . . . blast it . . . somebody clouted me on the head." Sparks's knobby fingers explored the back of his skull. He winced. "Got a good-sized goose egg back there, too."

Fargo realized that even without the glare of the flames, it was light enough in the alley to see fairly well. That meant the sun would soon be up. He and Washburn had intended to be on the trail about now. Fargo glanced at the damaged wagon. That wasn't going to happen.

And he was pretty sure he knew who to blame for that.

"Did you see who hit you?" he asked Sparks.

Sparks shook his head, then winced again at the pain caused by the movement. "Nope, didn't see a thing. Didn't hear anything, either."

It was hard to imagine either Lucius or Malachi Reese being able to sneak up on Sparks so successfully. They were too noisy for that. But Isaac Reese might have been able to, or Susannah. After what had happened the night before, he wasn't going to put anything past her.

He put a hand under Sparks's arm. "We'd better find a doctor to take a look at you."

"No need for that," Sparks said as Fargo helped him to his feet. "Takes a lot to dent this old noggin of mine."

"Are you sure?"

"Yeah. Gimme a cup of coffee and I'll be fine."

Fargo looked at one of the townies standing in the alley. "Will you take him over to the hotel and see that he gets some coffee?"

"Sure, mister," the man replied. He took Sparks's arm and steered him out of the alley.

Fargo joined Washburn next to the wagon. The freighter was examining the damage. Nearly half the canvas cover was gone, burned away and the top sideboard was charred badly along its edge. Surprisingly, except for a few small burned spots where embers had landed on them, the boxes and bags that contained the load of supplies didn't seem to be harmed.

"It might've been a lot worse if I had come along a couple of minutes later," Washburn said. "If the fire had gotten a better hold, it would have taken the whole wagon and everything in it."

"I'm sure that's what they intended."

Washburn looked over at Fargo. "Reese and his bunch?"

"Nobody else has any reason to want to burn your wagon, do they?"

Washburn shook his head and said, "Nope, nary a soul. Do we call the law on them?"

"Unfortunately, knowing something and being able to prove it to a lawman are two different things," Fargo pointed out. "Sparks didn't see who hit him. I'll ask around while you're seeing about getting this damage repaired, but I doubt if I'll turn up any witnesses who saw what happened, either."

"You're right, Fargo," Washburn said with a sigh. "All we can do is get this fixed and go ahead. Shouldn't take too long to replace the sideboard and get some new canvas stretched over the back. We won't be delayed by more'n a couple of hours." He added with some satisfaction, "That ought to disappoint Reese."

Major Gilmore strode into the alley. He looked at the

damaged wagon and exclaimed, "My God, what happened here?"

It seemed pretty obvious to Fargo, but he didn't point that out. Instead, he said, "Somebody attacked our guard and tried to burn the wagon."

"Is the man all right?" Gilmore asked.

Fargo gave the officer a little credit for inquiring about Sparks's health before anything else. "He will be."

"What about the wagon?"

Washburn said, "We can fix it. Shouldn't take too long, Major. We'll be on the trail before the morning's over."

"That's good," Gilmore said, "because you'll need all the time you can get if you're going to make Fort Phantom Hill in a week."

Washburn frowned. "You're not going to hold this delay against us, are you, Major? This wasn't our fault."

"If you get that contract, a great many unforeseen things can happen. The army needs to be sure that you can still deliver on time, Mr. Washburn, despite any setbacks."

Fargo saw Washburn's face flush angrily. "Damn it, that ain't—" Washburn began.

Fargo stepped in. He knew Washburn was going to say that wasn't fair, and he agreed with the freighter. But Major Gilmore didn't care about being fair. He just cared about what was best for the army. Fargo said, "We'll make it, Major."

"I hope you do," Gilmore said, and he sounded sincere. Fargo knew better than to put too much stock in that, however.

Now that the early morning excitement was over, the crowd had drifted away. Fargo did as he'd said he would, asking around town if anyone had seen anything suspicious around the alley. Just as he'd thought, no one had. Reese was going to get away with it.

This time. Fargo vowed that the next time would be different.

When he got back to the alley, he found that Washburn had already removed the burned sideboard and replaced it with a new one from the lumberyard down the street. Sparks was back, too, and the two men were stretching a new canvas cover over the curved wooden hoops in the back of the wagon and tying it in place.

"How are you doing, Sparks?" Fargo asked the old man.

"Right as rain," Sparks said. "Told you it'd take more'n one clout to dent this old skull o' mine."

"I'll go down to the livery to fetch the team in a few minutes," Washburn said. "Want me to tell the hostler to saddle up that Ovaro of yours, Fargo?"

"I'll take care of that myself, right after I try to get some breakfast again."

Washburn chuckled. "Yeah, you keep missin' meals on account of me, don't you?"

"No, I blame Reese."

"That's one more good reason to hate the son of a bitch."

Fargo couldn't argue with that.

He was able to finish his meal this time, and he felt pretty good as he came back to the alley a short time later, leading the now-saddled Ovaro. The horse was full of his usual high spirits this morning, ready to hit the trail. So was Fargo. He had ridden through the Brazos River country before, but it had been a while and he was eager to see it again.

The damage was repaired and the wagon was ready to roll. Washburn and Sparks sat on the driver's box. Washburn held the reins. "All set, Fargo?" he called.

Fargo swung up into the saddle and nodded. "All set." He turned the Ovaro and started west along Fort Worth's main street toward the bluff and the Trinity River beyond it.

Getting the fully loaded wagon down the steep bluff trail was trickier than driving up it with an empty wagon, but Washburn managed with the skill of a born teamster. The wagon rolled across the bridge and along the trail that had brought them to Fort Worth from O'Bar. After a few hundred yards, another trail curved off to the left, leading in a more westerly direction.

Some twenty miles west of Fort Worth was a small settlement called Weatherford, Fargo knew. About the same distance beyond Weatherford lay an even smaller community known as Golconda. Beyond that, there wasn't much of anything except a few isolated farms and ranches until Fort Phantom Hill. That wasn't even the official name of the fort; it was carried on army records as "Post on the Clear

Fork of the Brazos." But people had discarded that unwieldy title and referred to it by the name derived from the windswept knoll on which the fort sat. At one time the post had housed two full companies of infantry. Fargo thought the garrison was smaller than that now, but he wasn't sure about that. The fact that the army was trying to set up a better supply line to the fort using a civilian contractor implied that more troops might be sent there in the future.

That was the way of it, Fargo thought as he rode along a short distance ahead of the wagon. The troops came, gradually pushing back the line of the frontier. About the same time, ranchers moved in, hardy souls willing to risk some danger if it meant a chance to establish a cattle empire. Behind the soldiers and the ranchers were the farmers, and on their heels were the townspeople who served their needs. Before you knew it, there were settlements scattered all across the country, and although there were still the sort of wild, untamed places that called out to men like Fargo, they were fewer and farther between.

He didn't hate civilization, as some of the first men to come to the West did now that it was finally catching up to them. That was just part of the process of life, the never-ending cycle that began with barbarism on one end and progressed to stagnation and decay and the inevitable fall to a new barbarism on the other. Fargo recognized the process without necessarily embracing it, and he would play his part in it as fate ordained. There was nothing else a man could do.

He didn't have to scout ahead on this stretch of the journey. The trail, though narrow, was laid out clearly. It paralleled the Trinity River for several miles before the river curved to the north. There was a ford where the wagon could cross the stream. A few miles farther on, they passed a small cluster of log cabins, a community known as White Settlement. Beyond that they entered a stretch of rolling hills dotted with trees and crossed by creeks. This terrain ran all the way to Weatherford, Fargo recalled from his last trip to the area. Past that, the landscape became rockier and more rugged, and the woods were thicker.

From time to time he dropped back alongside the wagon to chat with Washburn and Sparks. Both of them were quite talkative, but their conversation revolved around different subjects. It turned out that Washburn often had bizarre, vivid dreams, and he seemed to enjoy describing them in great detail. Sparks talked mostly about places he had been and trails he had taken. Like Fargo, he had been over most of the major trails in the West. Fargo enjoyed talking to both of them. Like many Westerners, he had spent great stretches of time in his life alone. Good company was something precious on the frontier.

Fargo wasn't so distracted by the conversation, however, that he failed to do his job. Washburn might not need his scouting ability right now, but Fargo's keen eyes constantly scanned the landscape around them for any sign of trouble. Isaac Reese had made it plain he would stop at nothing to prevent Washburn from reaching Fort Phantom Hill in time to secure that government contract.

No one seemed to be following them, Fargo noted as he checked their back trail, nor were there any warning signs of an ambush. But it was only a matter of time, Fargo told himself. Every attempt Reese or his children had made to stop Washburn had failed, but Reese wouldn't give up.

Fargo had hoped they would reach Weatherford before nightfall, but the late start due to the fire prevented that. As darkness settled down over the land, they had no choice but to stop and make camp.

"Think it's safe to have a fire?" Washburn asked. "I haven't heard of any Indians raiding this far east for quite a while."

"Neither have I," said Fargo, "but it's still possible. Keep the fire small, and we'll put it out as soon as we've heated up some supper."

Washburn had put some beans on to soak in an iron pot before leaving Fort Worth that morning. He cooked them over the small campfire that Sparks built, chopping several wild onions into the pot as well. While the beans were cooking, Washburn made some corn bread. When the food was done, Sparks threw sand on the fire to put it out, and then the three of them sat down in the dark to eat. As his part of the chores, Fargo had tended to the Ovaro and the wagon team, unhitching the draft horses and hobbling them so they wouldn't wander off. He didn't have to worry about that where the Ovaro was concerned. The big black-and-white paint stallion wouldn't stray far from him and couldn't be taken away without a fight.

The food was good, and Fargo said as much. Washburn chuckled. "It's the onions that do it," he declared. "Got to have plenty of onions in the beans to make 'em good."

"I remember I had some mighty good beans up in Kansas once," Sparks said. "Or was it Missouri? I was on my way somewhere . . . Now where in blazes was it I was goin'? Anyway, these beans had molasses cooked in with 'em."

"Molasses is good in beans," Washburn agreed solemnly. "Not as good as onions, though."

"You can't put onions in everything."

"Why not?"

"I don't reckon onions in peach cobbler would be very good."

"Well, hell, what kind of damn fool would put onions in peach cobbler in the first place?"

"I didn't say anybody would, I just said it wouldn't be very good."

"Now, a stew, you got to put onions in that."

"Best stew I ever had was out in California, at a mining camp up in the Sierra Nevadas. You never saw such a road as you had to go over to get to the place."

Fargo just grinned in the darkness and ate his supper.

The night passed peacefully, which came as a bit of a surprise to Fargo. He had halfway expected Isaac Reese to make another attempt to kill them or at least destroy the wagon. When the sun rose, however, they were back on the trail, rolling toward Weatherford.

They passed through the little settlement at midmorning, noting several wild peach trees in the area that were loaded down with ripe fruit. Some fine peaches grew out here, Fargo recalled. He plucked one from a tree as he rode past. He stopped at a creek, washed the prickly fuzz off the fruit, and bit into it. Sweet juices filled his mouth. The peach tasted so good he wished he had picked some more.

A range of small hills rose to the west of Weatherford. Fargo didn't think the wagon would have any trouble getting through them, but the time had come for him to find the best trail. He reined the Ovaro to a halt and waited until the wagon pulled up alongside him.

"Keep going in this general direction," Fargo told Washburn. "I'm going to have a look up in those hills."

Washburn nodded in agreement. "Probably a good idea. I think this trail we're on is goin' to peter out in a while."

Fargo thought the same thing. "I'll be back in a couple of hours," he said as he lifted a hand in farewell.

He heeled the Ovaro into a ground-eating trot. As the horse stretched its legs, Fargo could tell that the stallion wanted to run. He gave the Ovaro its head for a few minutes, and both of them enjoyed the gallop. When Fargo reined the paint back to a trot and glanced over his shoulder, he saw that the wagon was now out of sight.

The trail they had been following did indeed come to an end, Fargo discovered as he spent the next hour riding into the hills. But most of the slopes were gentle enough so that the wagon could negotiate them without much trouble. He had to ride along several creeks until he located places where the banks were low enough for the wagon to ford. Fargo made a mental note of the locations of those fords and knew he would never forget them. That was one of the things that made him the Trailsman: the ability to look at a landscape and instantly, permanently, absorb all of its features.

He emerged from the hills onto a long, flat stretch of ground bordered by more hills to the north and reined the Ovaro to a halt. It was time to turn back and rejoin Washburn and Sparks. They would just about be reaching the eastern edge of the hills, Fargo estimated. Once he got back to them, he knew he would have no trouble leading them through.

Now that he had scouted the best path, he rode more quickly. The sun was high in the sky. Once the wagon crossed through the hills, he thought, they could make good time on that flatland. They might even be able to make up the time they had lost the day before. Fargo hoped that by nightfall they would be at least forty miles west of Fort Worth. They needed to be, if they were going to have any chance of covering the distance to Fort Phantom Hill in the allotted time.

During his ride, Fargo had seen tendrils of smoke from

**60**

the chimneys of isolated cabins, but those were the only signs of human habitation. He hadn't seen any other riders or wagons. But as he started up one of the steeper hills, a series of faint popping sounds came to his ears. Fargo stiffened in the saddle as he heard them.

*Gunshots.*

Fargo hesitated only a split second as he realized that the shots were coming from the east, from the direction where Washburn and Sparks were. Then he put the Ovaro into a gallop and surged up the hill, a bleak look in his eyes.

Reese had waited until he was gone to strike, Fargo thought. He believed it was safe to attack the wagon and the two men with it.

He was about to find out different.

=========== **7** ===========

The Ovaro topped the rise with Fargo leaning forward in the saddle. The slope fell away fairly steeply on the far side. At the bottom twisted the creek that had formed this little valley. Its banks were thickly grown with post oaks and live oaks. Fargo saw a haze of powdersmoke floating over the treetops.

The shooting was still going on. The sharper cracks of rifles were punctuated by the dull, hollow roar of a scattergun. That would be Sparks, Fargo guessed as he rode toward the creek. The old man probably wasn't doing much good with that greener. Likely the bushwhackers had set up their ambush so that they were out of shotgun range.

Fargo didn't know how much intelligence to give Isaac Reese credit for. Would Reese have thought to set out a sentry, in case Fargo came back before the attack was over? Or would he have thrown all his firepower into the ambush? Fargo didn't know Reese well enough to answer that question.

But a moment later he got a pretty good indication when something small and deadly whipped past his ear. He felt the concussive wind of the bullet's passage through the air. He swerved the Ovaro to the left and hunkered down lower in the saddle, making himself a smaller target.

As he raced toward the creek, he wrapped his right hand around the stock of the Henry rifle and slid it from its fringed sheath strapped to the saddle under his left leg. The magazine was fully loaded, but Fargo kept the chamber empty when he was traveling. He took hold of the breech with his left hand, the same hand that was holding the Ovaro's reins, and used his right to work the rifle's lever, jacking a round into the chamber.

Another shot buzzed past him. This time Fargo caught a glimpse of a muzzle flash under the trees to the right. He brought the Henry to his shoulder and snapped a shot in that direction, not expecting to hit anything. He just wanted to give the bushwhacker something to think about.

He veered the Ovaro again, this time to the right. That took him toward whoever was shooting at him, but sometimes it was more difficult to hit somebody galloping straight at you, rather than one who was moving at an angle. He fired the Henry again.

The shotgun blasted once more. Assuming that Sparks had the shotgun, and judging by the sounds of the other shots, Fargo decided that the bushwhackers had the wagon surrounded. They probably had struck while the wagon was fording the creek. Washburn and Sparks would have been concentrating on getting safely across the stream.

A third shot whined by Fargo's head, but again it was a clean miss. He reached the edge of the trees on the creek bank, kicked his feet free of the stirrups, and left the Ovaro's back in a rolling dive that sent his hat flying from his head. The impact jarred Fargo, but he was able to roll over and come up on his feet as the horse trotted on. Holding the Henry across his chest, Fargo planted his back against a tree trunk and waited to see what was going to happen.

He didn't have long to wait. A slug chewed bark from the trunk about a foot over his head. He saw the flash and a puff of smoke from a clump of undergrowth surrounding a fallen tree. Fargo fired, aiming just over the deadfall, and as the echoes of the shot faded, he was rewarded by a yelp of pain.

Fargo dropped to his knees and crawled several feet to another tree. More bullets tore through the brush around him, clipping leaves from the branches and snapping off limbs. He came up in a crouch and ran toward another fallen tree, one of many along the creek. When he got there he threw himself down behind it.

When he raised his head carefully and peered through the brush, he could see the wagon. It was stopped at the edge of the creek with the horses on the bank but the wheels still in the water. Fargo didn't see Washburn or Sparks on the driver's box. He counted four places on the canvas cover where bullets had ripped holes in it. There were probably others he couldn't see.

If Washburn and Sparks had been able to get in the back of the wagon before they were hit, there was at least a chance they were still all right. The sideboards were thick enough to stop most of the slugs, and the crates and bags of supplies in the back would also offer some protection. But the longer this battle went on, the greater the chances that one or both of the men would be wounded—or worse.

The shotgun roared again, with the sound definitely coming from the wagon. In addition, a rifle barked at regularly spaced intervals. It sounded like a single-shot Spencer, Fargo thought. He wasn't sure, but he believed Washburn carried just such a rifle in the wagon. The fact that two weapons were being fired in defense boded well.

On his belly again, Fargo used his elbows and toes to push himself to the end of the log. He looked around it carefully. Upstream from the ford, a thick tangle of brush stretched nearly all the way across the creek. Sometime in the past, a tree had fallen into the water, and broken branches and other debris washing downstream had hung up on it, forming a dam of sorts. As Fargo watched, he saw several puffs of smoke from the brush and heard the crackle of gunfire from that direction.

So that was one place the bushwhackers had lain in wait, he thought. He knew there were others around, but he had a good shot at these. That brush wouldn't stop a steel-jacketed slug from the Henry. Fargo opened fire, raking the clump of brush with five shots that he squeezed off as fast as he could work the rifle's lever.

As he expected, return fire tore into the log that shielded him. The bullets pulverized the rotten wood and threw it into the air as a cloud of splinters and dust that settled down around Fargo. He blinked his eyes clear as the dust stung them. If nothing else he had gotten the attention of the bushwhackers off the wagon for a few minutes.

When the fusillade stopped, Fargo still didn't move. Let them think they had gotten him, he told himself. That might draw them out. He waited patiently in motionless silence.

All the shooting had stopped now. From the wagon, a shout came. "Fargo? Is that you? You all right? Fargo!"

Fargo grimaced but didn't answer. He recognized Washburn's voice. It was necessary to let the freighter think he was dead or badly wounded.

No one else responded to Washburn's shout either. Fargo halfway expected Isaac Reese to taunt Washburn, but that didn't happen.

Quietly, Fargo edged forward enough to see the wagon. It shifted a little on its springs and thoroughbraces, as if someone were moving around inside. *Stay there!* Fargo thought. Surely Washburn and Sparks had enough sense to remain in the wagon.

Leaves crackled somewhere close by. Here under the tree, years' worth of fallen leaves had rotted into soft mulch, but a few of them were still brittle enough to make noise when they were stepped on. Fargo didn't breathe for several moments, concentrating all of his senses and waiting for another telltale sign that someone was trying to sneak up on him.

When another crackle came, it was even closer. Too close. Fargo's instincts sent him rolling away from the log as a pistol barked twice from downstream. Bullets thudded into the log.

Fargo's keen eyes spotted the man standing in a crouch a dozen feet away. The man's shirt was stained with blood on the left shoulder. He had to be the lookout Fargo had winged a few minutes earlier. Lying on his back, Fargo fired the Henry, worked the lever, and fired again. Both slugs punched into the man's chest and threw him backward. He flung his arms in the air as he fell. Dust and mold flew up around him as he landed heavily on the rotting leaves.

More shots rolled out like the rumble of thunder. Fargo heard the shrill scream of a horse in agony. Biting back a curse, he risked coming to his knees so that he could fire over the log. Seven shots remained in the Henry. He emptied them all into the brush that hid some of the bushwhackers. By the time he had done that, the white-hot rage that had filled him a second earlier was easing, and he had the presence of mind to go to ground again

He had a box of cartridges for the Henry in the Ovaro's saddlebags, but he carried a few extra shells in the pocket of his shirt, too. He dug them out and thumbed them into the rifle's loading gate.

The thudding of hoofbeats came faintly to Fargo's ears. Were the ambushers pulling out? It sounded like it, but Fargo suspected a trick. The hoofbeats faded away, and the woods along the bank of the creek were completely quiet now. All the animals had been frightened away by the shooting, so there weren't even the small, everyday noises to be heard. Long minutes crept past, seeming even longer.

Finally, when Fargo estimated that at least a quarter of an hour had gone by, he risked a look. He couldn't see anything moving around the clump of brush. Then, while he was watching, a bluejay landed on the fallen tree and began pecking at bugs in the rooted wood. The bird wouldn't have been doing that if any would-be killers were still concealed in the brush.

Fargo glanced at the man he had shot. Still no movement or other sign of life. Fargo was pretty sure he had taken the man down for good. That was a shame. He would have liked to have been able to try and get some questions answered. Unfortunately, there hadn't been time to get fancy with his shooting. If he had tried, it probably would have just gotten him killed.

He came up in a crouch and moved from tree to tree like a flitting shadow as he searched for any more gunmen who might have been left behind. He didn't find any bushwhackers, but he found one shell casing downstream that hadn't been picked up when the man who'd fired the shot had left hurriedly. The shell was from a Henry much like his own, Fargo decided.

He walked back to the dead man and looked down at him. The swarthy, bearded face was unfamiliar to Fargo. He was sure he had never seen the man before. He searched the man's pockets but found nothing except some grease-stained, wadded-up greenbacks. That was enough to convince Fargo that the man was a hired gun. There was nothing, however, to connect him positively to Isaac Reese.

So there was the rub again. Fargo knew Reese had been behind this attack, but he couldn't prove it. Not that there was any law out here to report it to. There would be a county sheriff back in Weatherford, but Fargo doubted if he would be interested in trying to track down the bush-whackers. Besides, Fargo, Washburn, and Sparks didn't have time for that. They had to push on if they wanted to make Fort Phantom Hill. Every delay could prove costly.

"Son of a bitch!"

The shout came from the creek and sounded like Washburn. He was angry, though, not scared or in danger. Leaving the dead man where he had fallen, Fargo walked over to the riverbank and saw Washburn and Sparks standing in the mud at the edge of the water, looking down at the body of one of the horses sagging in its harness. The other animals were made visibly nervous by the closeness of death.

Washburn looked up at Fargo. "When the bastards saw that they couldn't kill us, they went after the horses instead!"

Fargo nodded in agreement. "I'm surprised they didn't do that sooner. Killing your team would stop you from getting to the fort."

"Yeah, but Reese is greedy. He figured the horses would be worth something to him. If he could kill us and steal the horses, too, he'd come out ahead all the way around."

It would take a mighty callous man to look at the situation that way, Fargo thought, but Isaac Reese seemed to fit that description.

Fargo whistled, and the Ovaro came trotting out of the woods a moment later. Fargo was pleased to see that the big stallion was unharmed. The Ovaro had a knack for getting out of the way of stray bullets that served him well.

"We'll have to find another horse or a mule," Fargo said as he got the .44–.40 cartridges from his saddlebags and reloaded the Henry. He slid the rifle back in its sheath. "You can't get very far with an unbalanced team like that. In the meantime, we can hitch up my horse. He won't like it much, but he'll pull if he has to. Better make him one of the leaders, though. He's less likely to take a bite out of one of the others that way."

"Whatever you think, Fargo," Washburn said. "He's your stallion, so I reckon you know him better'n anybody else."

The next half hour was spent getting the harness loose from the dead horse, moving the wagon away from the carcass and onto the creekbank, and rehitching the team so that the Ovaro was the off leader. As Fargo finished buckling the harness in place, the stallion gave him a look that made Fargo chuckle. "Sorry, big fella," he said as he patted the Ovaro's neck. "Maybe it won't be for too long. I hope not."

"I'll ride in the back of the wagon so you and Paul can have the box," Sparks volunteered. He jerked a thumb toward the woods. "What're we goin' to do about that dead man? Just leave him there for the wolves?"

That sounded like a good idea to Fargo, but he knew he couldn't do it. "Break out the shovels," he said. "Burying is more than a bushwhacker deserves, but I suppose we'd better do it anyway."

When the dead man had been laid to rest in a shallow grave, Fargo and Washburn took their seats on the driver's box while Sparks climbed into the back of the wagon. Washburn handled the reins. He got the team moving, including Fargo's Ovaro, and the wagon rolled on, heading west.

Recalling perfectly the route he had mapped out earlier in his mind, Fargo told Washburn where to go. Fargo rode with the Henry in his lap, alert for any sign of another ambush. The miles rolled past peacefully, however. Isaac Reese must have given up for the time being. Fargo was convinced that the respite was only temporary. Reese wasn't the sort of man to admit defeat.

The wagon left the range of hills and started across the stretch of flatland. Fargo seemed to recall from previous trips to this part of the country that the flats ran all the way to the Brazos River, sloping gently down to the stream as they approached it. He had hoped to reach the Brazos today, but that wasn't likely to happen now.

The Ovaro was no draft horse. The stallion tried gallantly but lacked the raw power and stamina of the other horses. Capable of running all day with Fargo on his back, the paint found pulling a wagon tougher going. That slowed them down even more.

Late that afternoon, Fargo spotted a tendril of smoke rising off to the right. He pointed and said to Washburn, "That must be a farm. We might be able to buy another horse there."

"We'll give it a try," Washburn said as he swung the wagon in that direction. "Even if we can't replace that dead horse, I'm sure the folks will be hospitable. Might have a barn where we can sleep tonight."

Some shelter and a home-cooked meal sounded good to Fargo, too. A short time later, they came in sight of a log cabin built in the usual dogtrot style. The smoke they had seen rose from a stone chimney on the left side of the cabin. Beyond that was the barn that Fargo had hoped to see. There were plowed fields with crops growing in them. All the signs indicated that here was a place that might have a mule or a horse to spare.

As the wagon approached, a couple of kids ran from the barn to the cabin and ducked inside, probably frightened by the presence of strangers. A man emerged from the barn as well, but he wasn't running. He walked forward confidently, a rifle held in his hands. When the wagon was still about fifty feet away, he raised his voice and called, "That's far enough, gents!"

Washburn brought the team to a halt. He said, "Howdy! We ain't lookin' for trouble, mister."

"That's always good to hear." The man had a deep, educated voice that was somewhat at odds with his outfit of overalls, rundown boots, and broad-brimmed straw hat. "I can offer you water and something to eat, though the fare won't be fancy. There's grain in the barn for your animals. Light and set."

Fargo hopped down easily from the wagon seat. "We're obliged for the hospitality, Mister . . . ?"

"Andrews. Zach Andrews."

"My name is Skye Fargo. That's Paul Washburn on the box, and the old-timer looking over his shoulder is called Sparks. We're bound for Fort Phantom Hill with a load of supplies for the army."

"You're welcome to spend the night here," Andrews said. "Not much light left. You couldn't go much farther." He lowered the rifle to his side, holding it in his left hand. As he came forward, he extended his right and said, "I'm pleased to make your acquaintance, Mr. Fargo."

Fargo shook hands with him. "Likewise, Mr. Andrews. I'm glad to see you've decided that we mean no harm."

"Oh, I'm not totally convinced of that," Andrews said with a faint smile. "I'm just confident in my wife's shooting ability."

Fargo glanced toward the cabin and spotted the barrel of a rifle sticking out from a small gap between the shutters over one of the windows. He grinned. "It's a smart man who doesn't take too many chances out here. I reckon the boy you left in the barn is a good shot, too?"

Andrews returned the grin and said, "He's been able to knock down a squirrel at a hundred yards since he was six years old." He turned his head and called toward the barn, "Come on out, Ben. It's all right."

A lanky, dark-haired teenage boy emerged from the barn a moment later, cradling an old flintlock rifle in his arms. He regarded the visitors warily and said, "At least they're not Kiowas, Pa."

Fargo frowned a little at that comment. "You've had Indian trouble around here?"

"Not right now, not lately," Andrews replied. "Word is that the Kiowas have hit a couple of homesteads over in the Palo Pinto Hills, beyond the Brazos. We haven't seen any savages, but we've been keeping our eyes open." He looked at Washburn. "Bring that wagon on over to the barn, Mr. Washburn. We'll get your team unhitched. Sort of odd, seeing a paint horse like that pulling a wagon."

"That's another thing we'd like to talk to you about," Fargo said. "We're in need of a mule or a draft horse if you've got one you wouldn't mind selling."

Andrews rubbed his jaw, which had a day's worth of

beard stubble on it. "Well, I don't know about that. I've got an old mule I don't use much for plowing anymore, but he's not much count. Might not last much farther than that fort you're bound for."

"That's all we need," Washburn said. "I'll give you a mighty fair price, Mr. Andrews."

"We'll talk about it after supper," Andrews decided. "Come on, let's get you unhitched."

Fargo glanced at the cabin. The rifle barrel had been withdrawn from the window. Mrs. Andrews had made up her mind that the visitors were not a threat. Fargo was willing to bet that she was keeping an eye on them, however, just in case.

By the time night had fallen, Fargo and his two companions had met all five members of the Andrews family. The farmer's wife was named Emily. She was a slender, dark-haired woman, still pretty despite the hardships of frontier living The sometimes-harsh existence drained years and vitality from all but the strongest women. Fargo had a hunch Emily Andrews fell into that category. The two younger children were a boy about ten named Quint and a little girl of seven or eight called Susie. Both of them looked at Fargo with something like amazement in their eyes. Fargo figured out why when Quint said, "You wear buckskins like an Indian, mister."

"Quint . . ." Andrews said warningly.

Fargo grinned and hunkered down so that his eyes were on a level with Quint's as they stood in the dogtrot. "It's all right," he said to Andrews. To the boy, he said, "Buckskins hold up well, and once you've worn them for a while, they're pretty comfortable. And this fringe comes in handy sometimes if you need to mend a harness or something like that. The Indians have a lot of good ideas. I always figured a man could learn something from just about anybody, no matter what color he is or how he lives."

"I wouldn't want to learn how to scalp people," Quint said.

'Well, no, that's not a good thing," Fargo admitted. "But I'll bet you didn't know that the Indians learned how to do that from white men."

Quint's eyes widened "No!"

"Yep," Fargo said with a solemn nod. "They picked up

the habit from some of the French trappers who came across Canada and down into what's now the United States."

"Dang! I thought it was something just Indians did."

"Well, these days, that's right most of the time," Fargo said. "Although in some places white men still hunt Indian scalps, just like the other way around."

"That's enough talk about scalps," Emily Andrews said firmly. "Quint, you and Susie go wash up for supper, you hear me?"

"Yes'm," the little boy said as he and his sister scurried off.

Fargo straightened and looked at Mrs. Andrews. "I'm sorry if I spoke out of turn, ma'am."

"No, that's all right," she said. "This is still a violent land, for all its beauty. It doesn't hurt them to know the truth. I just didn't want the discussion going on around the dinner table."

Fargo smiled. "Can't blame you for that, ma'am."

They ate at a rough-hewn wooden table. Andrews said grace before they dug into the food. Sitting here like this, Fargo was reminded of the things that were missing from his life: a home and family, a sense of belonging somewhere. But any chance he'd had for such things was long gone, worn away by the years he had spent drifting all over the frontier. He knew, as well, that despite what he felt from time to time, he could never settle down. He was too restless for that, too eager to see what lay on the other side of the hill. A man who's been to see the elephant could seldom be content after that to stare at the hind end of a mule.

A mule was what was on Washburn's mind, however, specifically the mule that Andrews had indicated he might be willing to sell. The two men discussed the matter and agreed on a price. Fargo thought Washburn was paying more than the mule was worth, but their circumstances made it imperative they have another draft animal. Besides, Washburn insisted on the price; Andrews would have taken less.

When supper was over, the two younger children were sent to bed. Fargo, Washburn, Sparks, Andrews, and Ben went out into the dogtrot to sit and enjoy the evening air. It still held some of the heat of the day, but without the glare of the sun there was a welcome hint of coolness. Low down on the western horizon was a narrow band of reddish gold, the last surviving remnant of sunset.

"This is the best time of the day," Andrews said as he took out a pipe and began to pack tobacco in the bowl. "Makes all the hard work worthwhile."

"Amen," Washburn agreed. "You've got something worth hangin' on to here, Zach."

"I'll hang on to it," Andrews declared. "Come hell or high water. The Indians won't scare me off, and neither will the blue northers or the rattlesnakes or anything else the frontier can throw at us. We're here for good."

But it would be easier, Fargo thought, on Andrews and all the other settlers like him if the presence of the army brought peace to the land. Fargo might not particularly like the advance of civilization, but he realized that he was in the minority. A new supply route to Fort Phantom Hill was just the start, one more indication that things were changing for what most people would consider the better.

Fargo could live with that change, because when the time came he could always ride on. There would always be a frontier, at least in his lifetime.

But for now, he was content to sit there and enjoy watching the last of the sun's afterglow fade from the sky.

<hr>

# 8

<hr>

They were on their way early the next morning, with the mule that Zach Andrews had sold them now a part of the team pulling the wagon. Sometimes having a mule mixed in with a bunch of horses didn't work out too well, but as Washburn drove on toward the Brazos River, Fargo thought that the animals were getting along all right so far. As for Fargo, it felt good to be back in the saddle again after being forced to ride on the wagon the previous afternoon. And he knew by the way the Ovaro pranced along that the stallion was glad to be out of harness.

This flatland was more open, with fewer places where Isaac Reese could set up an ambush. Though still wary, Fargo wasn't as worried today about running into trouble. At midmorning, when his lake-blue eyes spotted what looked like the river valley several miles ahead of them, he felt confident enough that he decided to ride on ahead.

"I'll find a place we can ford the river," he told Washburn and Sparks. "The going gets more rugged on the other side, so make good time while you can out here on the flat."

Washburn nodded his agreement. "We'll keep our eyes peeled for Reese, too."

Sparks hefted the shotgun he had across his lap and laughed. "We'll give him a warm welcome if he comes callin'," he said.

Fargo recalled the way they had gotten pinned down by the bushwhackers the day before, but he didn't say anything. Washburn and Sparks would be careful. No need to point out past failures.

He let the Ovaro stretch its legs, and less than an hour later he was approaching the Brazos River. The flatland ran out about a mile east of the river, which was lined with wooded hills on both sides. The slopes weren't so steep, though, that the wagon couldn't manage them. Fargo rode down to the river and found a cutbank where the wagon could reach the water. By this point in the summer, the level of the river was usually down some, unless the spring rains had been unusually heavy. That hadn't been the case this year. The Brazos was flowing fairly well in its channel, but large sections of the stream bed were visible. Fargo rode out onto it, checking for sandbars where the wagon might get bogged down and looking for beds of gravel where crossing would be easiest.

The Ovaro swam through the channel without difficulty and emerged dripping on the western bank of the river. Fargo recalled that the Brazos was famous for twisting and looping back on itself in this region, so they might have to cross it two or even three times. He looked back toward the east, trying to estimate how long it would be before Washburn and Sparks arrived at the river. He decided there was time enough to ride on ahead and scout out the next crossing.

The hills were higher, more rugged and rocky on this side of the river. From some of the crests, he could see for miles. It was pretty country, some of the best that Texas had to offer. Not perfect for either ranching or farming but able to support either one.

Fargo topped a hill, and sure enough, there was the Brazos below him once again. He reined in and grinned. If a man didn't know the geography, he might think that he was losing his mind and living the same moment over again, because the river at this point looked almost identical to the way it was at the crossing earlier. There was an important difference, though. The banks were higher and steeper here, too high and steep for a wagon to make it up and down them. Someone had gotten around that problem by sinking pillars in the riverbed and building a plank bridge across the Brazos. That was new since the last time he had been here, Fargo thought.

He came to a faint trail that led to the bridge. This path had been traveled more heavily in the past than it was now. Fargo followed it, trotting the Ovaro along the heavily overgrown ruts. A few minutes later, he reached the river and the bridge that spanned it.

The bridge was open on the sides. Fargo dismounted and walked out onto it, checking for rotten planks. The bridge had deteriorated somewhat from disuse, but it still seemed sturdy enough. He found a few places that looked weak, but he thought they would hold up under the weight of the wagon. They'd just have to chance it, he thought.

Having walked all the way to the far end of the bridge, a distance of a little more than a hundred yards, Fargo stopped and turned around, intending to return to the Ovaro. He froze as he saw the men who had slipped out of the trees and now stood near the stallion, rifles in their hands. Even at this distance, he had no trouble recognizing Lucius and Malachi Reese. The last time he'd seen them, they had been dragging their battered bodies out of Fargo's hotel room in Fort Worth, after their attempt on his life had failed.

That made him think of Susannah. He wondered if she was somewhere close by, too.

Lucius Reese raised his voice and called, "Don't just stand there, Fargo! Get over here, you bastard!"

Fargo didn't know what they were up to, but he was sure it was no good. Equally certain was the fact that at this range, he couldn't hope to outduel a pair of rifles with nothing but a six-gun. His Henry was still in its saddle sheath.

Malachi leveled his rifle. "Damn you, get over here!" he shouted. "Or we'll kill you where you stand!"

Fargo sighed and started toward them. He had taken only a couple of steps, though, when he suddenly pursed his lips and let out a shrill whistle.

The Ovaro exploded into motion, lunging out onto the bridge and galloping toward Fargo. Lucius and Malachi yelled curses and started shooting. Fargo held his breath, hoping that none of the bullets would hit the stallion. The paint veered from side to side as much as he could on the narrow bridge, guided by instinct and the habits learned during years of running gunfights with Fargo on his back.

Fargo darted onto the bank and off to the side of the bridge. He palmed out his Colt and started blazing away at the Reese brothers, more to worry them than in hopes of actually hitting one of them. His bullets must have come close, because Lucius and Malachi abruptly stopped shooting and dived back into the woods that came nearly to the edge of the river.

The Ovaro had almost reached the western end of the bridge. Fargo jammed his revolver back in its holster and stepped toward the horse. He caught hold of the saddle horn and made a running mount, letting the horse's momentum pull him along for several steps before he was able to get his right foot in the stirrup and bounce off the ground. He swung his left leg over the stallion's back and settled down in the saddle.

It was at that moment when something struck him a heavy blow to the head. It felt as if a sledgehammer had crashed into his skull. He was driven forward over the neck of the horse and caught desperately at the Ovaro's mane in order to keep from tumbling off. Somehow he hung on, but his head was swimming now, and waves of blinding pain rolled through his brain. It was all he could do to stay on the horse.

Fargo didn't know it when he passed out. Blackness came up and swallowed him without him even being aware of it.

Pain was the first thing he knew when consciousness began to seep back into his body. Something was jabbing into the side of his face, and it was annoying the hell out of him.

Fargo tried to move way from the source of the irritation. He let out a groan as agony burst brightly inside his skull. He laid still for several minutes until the pain subsided somewhat. Then he tried once more to move, and this time he was prepared for what happened. He gritted his teeth, unwilling to give in to what he was feeling.

The pain in his cheek went away. Fargo realized he had been lying facedown on the ground. He blinked his eyes open and saw the broken twig that had been gouging the flesh of his face as he lay on it. He snaked a hand up, gently explored the spot of the injury with his fingertips. There was only a small spot of blood.

And his arm worked, too, which was a good sign. He wasn't completely paralyzed. He wiggled the fingers of his other hand, moved that arm as well. So both arms were all right. That left his legs.

He used his toes to push himself over onto his back. The maneuver served a twofold purpose. First, it told him that his legs responded to his mental commands, and second, it left him in position to sit up.

As he did so, at first he thought he had just made the worst mistake of his life. The world spun crazily around him, and he had to put both hands on the ground to steady himself. He hung on until the feeling began to pass after a few moments. His head still pounded, but at least he didn't feel quite as dizzy.

He heard a horse behind him. A second later, a wet nose nuzzled strongly against his shoulder. The Ovaro made a snuffling noise and then came around him. Fargo summoned up a bleak grin. "Glad you weren't Reese or one of his boys," he said. "Reckon if you were I'd have a bullet in the back of my head by now."

The horse snorted.

Fargo lifted his hand and touched the right side of his head, wincing as the contact made fresh darts of pain shoot through his brain. Lucius and Malachi must have been blazing away at him from the trees as he galloped off, and one of their bullets had kissed the side of his head. There was a welt just inside his hairline, but the skin was barely broken. The bump could have almost been mistaken for a bad mosquito bite.

That was one hell of a deadly mosquito, Fargo thought. Another inch to the right and he'd be either dead or mortally wounded.

But he wasn't, and Fargo had learned over the years not to dwell on what might have been. He stayed focused on what was.

Continuing his mental reconstruction of what had happened, he told himself that after the slug had grazed him, he had been able to stay in the saddle as the Ovaro galloped away from the river. The stallion was canny and would have known to take his master as far away from Lucius and Malachi as possible. Somewhere along the way, the unconscious Fargo had finally lost his grip and slipped from the back of the horse. When that happened, the Ovaro had stopped and stood guard over his senseless form.

Now that awareness had returned and Fargo was relatively certain what had happened, he looked around to see where he was. Dense growths of oak thickets lay on his right and left, but a narrow trail ran among the trees. Fargo had been lying at the edge of this trail.

He was a little surprised Lucius and Malachi hadn't come after him. Of course, it was possible that they had pursued but had been unable to find him. Either way, Fargo knew he had to get back to the Brazos and hook up again with Washburn and Sparks. What had happened to him was proof that the Reeses were still in the area and hadn't given up their quest to stop Washburn from reaching Fort Phantom Hill.

Fargo looked around until he spotted his hat lying on the ground nearby. He reached over, picked it up, and put it on. That made his head hurt again, but he forced himself to ignore the pain. He called the Ovaro over and gripped the stirrup to help haul himself to his feet. Once again, a wave of dizziness went through him. It wasn't as bad a the first one, though, and it passed quickly. Fargo's iron constitution gave him amazing recuperative qualities. A man had to be able to shake off his hurts in a hurry if he was going to survive on the frontier.

Fargo was about to pull himself into the saddle when he heard the voices. They were muffled by the thick growth all around him, and he didn't understand any of the words at first. He was sure, though, that the voices belonged to Lucius and Malachi Reese. A couple of seconds later, he heard the soft thudding of hoofbeats as horses came closer to him.

Moving quickly, Fargo led the Ovaro off the trail and forged a path for them into the deep shadows under the trees. The undergrowth closed behind them. After moving off the trail for several yards, Fargo stopped and turned back toward the path. He stood motionless beside the Ovaro, his hand on the stallion's muzzle to let him know to keep quiet.

From where he was, Fargo couldn't see the trail, but that was good. It meant that whoever rode along there couldn't see him, either. Lucius and Malachi were close now, close enough for him to be able to make out some of what they were saying.

"—hit that bastard in the head, I know I did." That was Malachi, Fargo thought, although he didn't know them well enough to be sure. Whichever one it was went on, "I seen him jerk in the saddle."

"That don't mean you hit him, you big lummox," the other one responded. "That horse of his sure as hell didn't slow down any."

"I still say I got him. We'll find him any minute now, a-layin' there on the ground with his brains blowed plumb out."

"You'd better hope so. Pa wants that damned Trailsman took care of before we blow up the other two."

Fargo tensed. *Blow up the other two?* What did that mean?

A chuckle came from one of the Reese brothers. "Those two old men'll be shocked when that bridge blows sky high around 'em. You reckon Pa's got enough blastin' powder?"

"Don't you worry about Pa. He can handle a charge of powder better'n . . ."

The voices faded away as Lucius and Malachi continued

their search for Fargo. They had no idea that they had just passed within yards of him.

Fargo's heart was pounding faster now, which made the ache in his head worse. He couldn't worry about that. He had overheard enough to know that Isaac Reese planned to blow up the bridge over the Brazos River while Washburn's wagon was on it. Blasting the bridge itself might be enough to prevent Washburn from reaching Fort Phantom Hill in time. Blowing it up with him and Sparks and the wagon on it would sure as hell do the job.

When he was confident that Lucius and Malachi were out of earshot, Fargo led the stallion back to the trail and swung up into the saddle. He tipped his head back, hoping to catch a glimpse of the sun through the trees so that he could orient himself. He had no idea how long he had sprawled there beside the trail, out cold. Surely by now Washburn and Sparks had had time to reach the first crossing of the Brazos. Would they find the second crossing— and the bridge—on their own? If they did, Fargo had to get back there and warn them before they started across the river.

The sun was fairly low in the sky, he saw to his dismay. That meant it was late afternoon. He had been unconscious for a while. Muttering under his breath, he headed the Ovaro back east along the twisting trail.

The shadows under the trees grew thicker as the afternoon drifted toward dusk. Wherever possible, Fargo put the stallion into a trot, even though the faster pace made his headache worse. He couldn't worry about things like that, not with the lives of two men at stake.

Finally, he came to the broad gap in the trees that marked the passage of the river. Fargo stopped, dismounted, and led the Ovaro into the brush again. Leaving the horse where it would stay ground-hitched for the time being, Fargo made his way on foot toward the Brazos, using all his skill to move silently and unobtrusively through the woods. A few minutes later, he came out on the bank of the river.

The bridge was below him and to the right, maybe twenty-five yards away. Fargo crouched beside a bush to study the situation.

He saw a few birds and squirrels moving around in the

trees along the riverbank, but that was the only sign of life. For a few moments, the apparent normality of the scene lulled him into thinking that Lucius and Malachi had been wrong about their father's plans. Isaac Reese might have intended to blow up the bridge, but it seemed that he was nowhere around here.

Then Fargo's eyes intently scanned the bridge itself, and his bearded jaw tightened as he spotted the small wooden keg lashed to one of the support beams almost exactly halfway across the bridge.

Fargo could see only a small part of the keg. The beam to which it was attached hid most of it. From downstream, however, the keg would be more visible—visible enough for a good shot to draw a bead on it and fire a rifle bullet into it, setting off the blasting powder inside. Using a fuse would be too unreliable and difficult to time. If Reese was sitting somewhere downstream, concealed in the brush along the bank, he could wait until the wagon with Washburn and Sparks was directly over the keg of blasting powder before firing. The resulting explosion would be immediate—and deadly.

His best bet was to locate Reese and stop the man from setting off the explosion, Fargo decided. That would require working his way silently along the bank, past the bridge, and using all of his skill to find Reese in time to stop him. But how far downstream would Fargo have to go to locate him? What if Reese was on the other side of the river?

While Fargo was turning over those questions in his head, the decision was taken out of his hands. Movement on the far side of the Brazos caught his eye, and he lifted his gaze to the bluff that sat a couple of hundred yards back from the river. The trail leading to the bridge ran down that bluff, and at the top of it, the wagon had appeared. Fargo saw Washburn and Sparks on the seat, looking tiny at this distance. They would reach the river in five minutes or less.

No time to search for Reese now, Fargo told himself. He had to get over there and warn his two friends. He could get the Ovaro and gallop across the bridge, stopping Washburn before the wagon reached the river.

But if he did that, Reese probably would guess that Fargo was on to his scheme, and he would go ahead and blow the bridge. That would leave Washburn and Sparks alive and the wagon intact, but they wouldn't be able to cross the river here. Who knew how long it would take them to find a place where they could ford? They could easily lose half a day or more.

A plan sprang into Fargo's mind. It was more dangerous, but if it worked, they would at least have a chance to continue on to Fort Phantom Hill.

Acting even as the plan formed, Fargo raced back to where he had left the Ovaro. He jerked his Henry from its sheath and ran upstream. The Brazos flowed around a bend a short distance to the north. When Fargo figured he was out of sight of the spot where Reese was hidden, he slid down the bank, splashed through the shallows, and waded quickly across the river's channel, holding the rifle and his six-gun in one hand over his head as he did so. Then he slogged through the sand and gravel of the riverbed until he reached the eastern bank.

Then it was a race, himself against the wagon. The brush slowed Fargo down somewhat, but he still moved quickly. He thought he heard the creak of wagon wheels over the pounding of his heart.

He burst out of the brush at the head of the bridge, just as the wagon reached it. Fargo grabbed hold of the tailgate and swung up. The added weight made the wagon shift, and Sparks twisted around on the seat, bringing up his scattergun in case whoever had just jumped onto the wagon was an enemy.

"It's me!" Fargo yelled to the two men. "Whip up the team, Paul! Get across as fast as you can!"

Even as Fargo shouted instructions, he was clambering over the load of supplies in the wagon. As he reached the opening at the front of the vehicle, he aimed the Henry past Washburn's shoulder.

Washburn was startled, but he responded to Fargo's order, bellowing at the team and flapping the reins against their backs. The horses and the lone mule broke into a run. The wagon swayed a little as it lurched out onto the bridge.

The Henry's magazine was full. Fargo fired five times, shifting his aim a little with each shot so that the bullets raked the western bank of the river. Somewhere along there was the most likely place for Reese to be hiding.

All he wanted to do was rattle Reese and throw off the man's aim.

The wagon bounced over the rough planks. It had covered twenty yards so far, about a fifth of the distance across. Suddenly, the heavy boom of a gunshot came from downstream. Fargo, who had carried a Sharps himself in the past, knew the sound of a high-caliber buffalo gun. He glanced ahead and saw splinters leap from the end of one of the planks as a heavy bullet chewed into it. Reese was using a Sharps to try to set off the blasting powder.

Fargo smiled tightly. The Sharps was a single-shot weapon. That would slow down Reese's rate of fire. He would have time for only a couple of more shots before the wagon passed beyond the keg of blasting powder. Fargo threw a pair of shots from the Henry toward the spot where the sound of the buffalo gun had come from. Ducking those bullets would slow down Reese even more.

"Keep 'em moving!" Fargo shouted to Washburn. There was no time now to worry about weak spots on the bridge. They would have to trust to luck on that score.

The Sharps boomed again. Fargo didn't see where the bullet went, but the blasting powder didn't go up so he knew the shot had been a miss. He fired twice more toward the area of the riverbank where he thought Reese was hidden.

The wagon raced past the midway point of the bridge. The keg of blasting powder was behind them now, Fargo thought. But if it went off while they were too close, it could still be deadly. "Go! Go!" he called to Washburn.

The freighter was shouting at his team at the top of his lungs. "Run, you sons o' bitches! Run—"

Suddenly, the world exploded into fire and noise not far behind the wagon. Fargo was thrown forward, slamming into the backs of Washburn and Sparks. He grabbed Sparks to keep the slender old man from being knocked off the wagon by the impact. Debris pelted the wagon. For a split-second, Fargo had the impression that the rear wheels were suspended in midair, blown up off the bridge by the force of the explosion. He never knew if that was true or not. But then, with a lurch and a jolt, all four wheels were definitely on the planks. The team kept running, and a moment later the wagon reached the end of the bridge and bounced onto the rutted trail. The woods closed in around them.

Fargo put a hand on Washburn's shoulder. "Keep going!" he said. "Put as much ground as you can between you and the river! I'll catch up later!"

Washburn glanced over his shoulder. "Fargo? Where are you go—"

By then, Fargo was moving to the back of the wagon. He swung his legs over the tailgate and dropped to the trail. Momentum spilled him off his feet, but he recovered quickly. He wasn't far from where he had left the Ovaro. He bulled through the undergrowth until he found the horse a moment later. The stallion seemed glad to see him. Fargo was pretty glad himself. He had just come too blasted close to being blown to bits.

He swung up into the saddle and turned the horse toward the trail. He would follow Washburn and Sparks and make sure that Reese didn't come after them, fighting a rearguard action if he had to.

But as he galloped after the wagon, there was no sign of Reese or anyone else. Reese had made another attempt to stop them—to kill them—and again he had failed. Would he admit defeat now and give up?

Fargo didn't think so. He rode toward the setting sun, knowing there was still trouble at his back.

# 9

Fargo hung back, making sure there was no pursuit and not trying to catch up to the wagon until he was satisfied that Reese wasn't coming after them. Then he let the Ovaro run, and within half an hour, the wagon came into view. The shadows were thick now. Soon they would have to make camp for the night.

Fargo came up with the wagon, the stallion easily cutting the gap. Washburn looked over at him and asked, "What the hell happened back there?"

"Reese had a keg of blasting powder planted under that bridge," Fargo explained. "He was going to set it off with a rifle shot while you were right over it."

Even in the dusk, Fargo could tell that both Washburn and Sparks paled at that news. Sparks said, "And you sent us out onto the bridge anyway?"

"I figured it was better to be on this side of it than stuck on the other side," Fargo said. "I knew if I started blazing away at Reese, I'd rattle him enough so that he'd miss his first couple of shots."

Washburn took a bandanna from his pocket and mopped sweat from his face. "Yeah, that's what happened, all right," he said. "But if Reese had hit that powder . . ."

Fargo nodded. "We'd all be playing harps about now."

"I sort of wish I'd never found that trail," Washburn muttered. "But I reckon you're right. It's over and done with now, and Reese still hasn't stopped us. He's got to be gettin' mighty frustrated."

"I'd sure like to get a good look at him over the sights o' this greener of mine," Sparks put in. "I'd bust his britches good with a load of buckshot."

"You may still get your chance," Fargo told him. "I don't think he'll give up just yet."

"Not hardly," Washburn agreed with a shake of his head. "Reese don't like gettin' beat, especially when it's going to cost him money."

They moved on west until it was too dark to see where they were going. Then Washburn pulled the wagon to a halt. They unhitched the team and made a cold camp. A fire and a hot meal would have been nice, but Fargo didn't want to advertise their location to Reese.

Not only that, but dark, thickly wooded hills now loomed all around them. They had reached the edge of the Palo Pinto Hills of which Zach Andrews had spoken. If Andrews was right, bands of marauding Kiowas had raided over here in recent weeks. That was another reason not to build even a small fire.

As the three men sat around gnawing jerky and stale biscuits, Fargo commented, "You didn't really need me to guide you, Paul. You're doing a good job finding the trails yourself."

Washburn grunted. "I've been durned lucky so far. And without your gun we'd be dead by now. This is twice you've pulled our fat out of the fire, Fargo. I'm much obliged."

"I don't like Reese," Fargo said. "I don't want to see him win."

His mind went back to Susannah Reese and the visit she had paid to his Fort Worth hotel room. Had her father sent her and her brothers there? Susannah had never really said so. In fact, she had denied that Reese even knew she was there. But the fact that she had let her brothers into the room to attack Fargo meant that he couldn't trust anything she had to say. From what he had seen so far, he didn't figure that Isaac Reese would hesitate at using his daughter's body to get what he wanted.

Still, despite what had happened before and after, there had been a moment when Fargo had sensed something genuine in Susannah's passion. No matter what had brought her to his bed, her longing, her desire, had been real. Fargo was certain of that.

He thought about the two women he had most recently bedded, Susannah Reese and Maddie Jenkins. They were a lot different. Maddie had been sweet and tender, yet possessed of a core of steely determination that had allowed her to make a life for herself on the frontier after the death of her husband. Susannah was much more fiery and outspoken, but she had withdrawn into herself when her father snapped at her back in Fort Worth. Despite her rougher exterior, there was a tentativeness to Susannah that was not to be found in Maddie. Maddie knew what she wanted, even when circumstances wouldn't always allow her to get it. Susannah probably thought she was sure of herself, but in reality she wasn't.

Fargo leaned back against one of the wagon wheels and grinned in the darkness. A man could spend his entire lifetime pondering the mysteries of the female mind and personality, he thought, but at the end he wouldn't be a damned bit closer to figuring anything out than when he started. Might as well ask yourself why the sky was blue or why the whippoorwill's song was so sad and so sweet at the same time.

They took turns standing guard all night, but there was

no trouble, no sign of Reese or his sons or his hired gunmen. Early the next morning, when dawn was just graying the eastern sky, the wagon was on the move again.

The trail they were following petered out in the hills. The slopes were so thickly wooded that even after the sun rose, the valleys were filled with shadows. Fargo led the way, finding the easiest paths for the wagon to take. However, the going was slow at best.

By late afternoon, they were still moving through the hills. Fargo wasn't sure how many miles they had covered today. The route they had been forced to follow had twisted and turned so much that it made distances impossible even to estimate. Fargo wasn't optimistic, though. They were four days out of Fort Worth, and he didn't think they were more than halfway to Fort Phantom Hill. At this rate the journey would take eight or maybe even nine days. Major Gilmore had given them a well-nigh impossible task to complete.

No one was ready to give up, though, especially after an entire day in which Isaac Reese had not tried to stop them. The attitude in camp that night was pragmatic, yet still cautiously optimistic.

"We'll give it our best shot," Washburn declared. "I'll be damned if we won't."

"One of these days there'll be roads all over this country," Sparks said. "Then a fella can get where he's goin' in a hurry. May not any of us live to see it, but mark my words, it's comin'." He sighed. "It'll get so crowded a man won't even be able to step out on his back porch to take a piss without the neighbors watchin'."

Fargo wasn't sure he wanted to live to see that day.

They got another early start the next morning. Fargo rode a little farther ahead this time, hoping to come to the end of the rugged range of hills.

Instead, he found himself once more sitting on the Ovaro high atop a bluff overlooking the Brazos River. Fargo grinned wearily. When the wagon came through here, this would make their third crossing of the river. The Brazos was proving to be a major obstacle between Fort Worth and Fort Phantom Hill. If Washburn got the freight contract from the army, he could rebuild the bridge that Reese had blown up. He might even want to build a bridge at the first crossing. This third one could prove to be more of a problem. The bluff dropped off almost sheer to the water, with no way for a wagon to get up and down it, and it ran as far north and south as Fargo could see. There was nothing he could do except start scouting for a better place to cross, going first one way and then the other if necessary.

He turned and rode south along the bluff, knowing that in general the terrain was less rugged in that direction. After a couple of miles, he hadn't found a place where the wagon could get down to the river. If he was the sort to get discouraged, he'd be feeling that way about now. Instead, he kept on searching with dogged determination.

Finally, after another mile or so, the bluff began to taper down toward the water. Fargo followed it and within a quarter of a mile came to a spot where Washburn would have no trouble driving the wagon right into the river. Fargo rode out into the Brazos, checking the channel and the riverbed. He nodded in satisfaction. The crossing could be made here.

He returned to the eastern bank of the river and turned north. Washburn would be steering as close to due west as was possible. Fargo hoped to intercept the wagon before it reached the bluff overlooking the Brazos, but if he didn't, he was confident that he would find Washburn and Sparks there waiting for him. There was nothing else they could do.

It was a beautiful summer day. Fargo knew from the way the air was heating up already that it would be a scorcher come late afternoon. A few white, fluffy clouds left over from early morning dotted the blue sky. Later in the day those clouds would be gone and the sky would turn hot and brassy, like pale silver. Fargo was going to enjoy them while they lasted. He was a man who took his pleasures where and when he could.

He was jogging along on the Ovaro when he heard the gunshots in the distance.

*Damn it, not again!* Fargo thought. There should have been two of him, one to scout the trails and one to stay with Washburn and Sparks and keep them out of trouble. He heeled the Ovaro into a run.

The bluff that paralleled the river was fairly open, without a lot of trees to slow Fargo down. The Ovaro stretched its legs into a ground-eating gallop. Guns kept popping somewhere up ahead. Fargo leaned forward in the saddle, urging more speed out of the stallion.

The Ovaro answered the call. Within minutes, Fargo spotted the wagon, up ahead and off to the right, bouncing and careening toward the river. The team was running full speed, out of control despite the figure on the box who sawed at the reins and shouted at the horses and the single mule. Fargo thought that was Sparks on the box, but he wasn't sure. He didn't see Washburn.

Maybe a hundred yards behind the wagon, half a dozen riders galloped in hot pursuit, banging away futilely with revolvers. At that range, they weren't going to hit anything with handguns, but they might not care about that. If they could keep the wagon team stampeding as it was now, it would soon plunge off the bluff and plummet forty or fifty feet into the Brazos River.

Grim-faced, Fargo angled the stallion so that he could intercept the wagon as far from the river as possible. His mind flashed back to his first meeting with Paul Washburn. He'd had to stop a runaway team there in O'Bar before the wagon crashed, and now here he was, days later and miles away, trying to do the same thing. Obviously, stampedes were a favorite tactic of the Reeses.

Despite the fact that the hurricane deck of a galloping horse was the worst possible platform for aiming, Fargo whipped out the Henry and threw a couple of shots toward the men pursuing the wagon. Maybe he could make them veer off.

The riders came on, undeterred by Fargo's shots. He bit back a curse and replaced the rifle in its sheath. He could worry about making a stand once the wagon was stopped safely. Until then, nothing else really mattered.

Fargo was closing in on the wagon now. He glanced to the left, saw that the edge of the bluff was approximately seventy-five yards away. He pulled the Ovaro into a sharp turn that sent the stallion racing alongside the wagon. Sparks was indeed bouncing on the driver's box, tugging futilely on the reins. From the back of the wagon, Fargo heard the crack of Washburn's Spencer. The freighter had climbed back there and was firing over the tailgate, trying without much success to discourage the pursuit.

*Too close.* They were just too damned close to the bluff, Fargo realized. The ground was flashing underneath the wagon. It was going too fast for anyone to be able to stop it in time.

"Jump!" Fargo bellowed at Sparks. "Get off of there!"

Sparks glanced at him, the weathered old face filled with stubborn anger. Fargo could tell that Sparks didn't want to abandon the wagon. But he had no choice. Jumping would be dangerous, but staying with the wagon when it went off the bluff would be suicide.

Before Sparks could make up his mind, he suddenly jerked forward and dropped the reins. Fargo saw a bright red stain flower on the old man's left side. Sparks slipped off the seat and onto the floorboard, dazed by the bullet that had clipped him.

Fargo didn't think about what he had to do. He kicked his feet free of the stirrups and launched himself from the saddle. His hands caught hold of the side of the driver's box and closed on it in an iron grip. He drew up his booted feet, careful to keep them out of the spokes of the wheel that was spinning madly only a few inches away. Using all the sheer strength of his arms and shoulders, he hauled himself up onto the box.

Sparks was regaining his senses. Fargo reached down to grab his shirt and pull him up. The edge of the bluff was thirty yards away now. "Can you jump?" he shouted at Sparks.

The old man nodded. "I'll probably break my fool neck, but there ain't nothin' left to do!"

Fargo gave him a nod. Sparks moved to the edge of the seat and leaped, pushing himself out as far away from the wagon as possible. Fargo turned and called back into the wagon, "Washburn! Get out of there!"

Washburn had been firing over the tailgate, just as Fargo thought. He looked at Fargo and shook his head. His beefy face was taut with anger. "I can't!"

Fargo could tell by Washburn's expression that nothing was going to change the freighter's mind. That meant Fargo had to try to stop the wagon, hopeless though it appeared to be.

The reins were still lying on the floor of the driver's box where Sparks had dropped them. Fargo snatched them up and hauled back on them. The maddened horses ignored the pull of the harness. Fargo saw ugly-looking wounds on the rumps of a couple of the animals where bullets had burned across them. That was how Reese and his boys had started the stampede, Fargo thought.

They were closing in on the rim. When the horses got to the edge, they would probably try to stop, but they wouldn't be able to. Their momentum would carry them on over the brink, and so would the wagon. And that was going to happen in no more than a handful of heartbeats.

Fargo dropped the reins, vaulted over into the back of the wagon, and scrambled over the load of supplies. When he reached Washburn he bent and grabbed hold of the freighter. "Let me go, damn it!" Washburn howled as Fargo jerked him to his feet. Fargo ignored the protest. Still hanging on to Washburn, he lunged out and sent both of them tumbling over the tailgate.

At that instant, the horses reached the edge of the bluff and plunged, screaming, over it. The wagon shot out into empty space behind them and seemed somehow to hesitate there in midair for a split second before dropping after the horses. There was a huge splash far below as the wagon quickly joined the horses as it crashed into the Brazos.

Fargo didn't hear that. The impact as he and Washburn struck the ground drove all the air from his lungs and made him pass out for a second. Consciousness flooded back into him as he rolled over and over. He came to a stop, still half stunned, and lifted his head to see Sparks hobbling quickly toward him. Sparks was waving a hand and yelling something, but it took Fargo a couple of seconds to figure out what was going on.

Reese, his sons, and his hired killers were still coming on, galloping toward Fargo and Sparks. Fargo got to his feet somewhat shakily and looked round for Washburn. The freighter was several feet away, groggily trying to push himself onto his hands and knees. His rifle lay beside him.

Fargo snapped, "Get one of his arms!" at Sparks, and together they got hold of Washburn and lifted him to his feet. Fargo snatched up the Spencer. They might need it, if Washburn had any ammunition for it. Still supporting Washburn, Fargo and Sparks turned and ran toward the edge of the bluff. Bullets whined around them.

The bluff dropped off sharply, but it wasn't completely sheer, Fargo recalled. They might be able to get beneath the rim and use it for cover. When they reached the edge, he saw several rocky protuberances with stubborn, scrubby bushes growing around them. Fargo and Sparks lowered Washburn onto the nearest of the rough ledges, then slid down after him.

This narrow haven was only about five feet below the rim, so when Fargo stood up he was able to see over the bluff onto the plain that led up to it. Luckily, his Colt had stayed in its holster during all the leaping about he'd been forced to do. He palmed out the gun and thumbed off a couple of shots at the onrushing attackers. Isaac Reese was in the lead, his duster flapping out behind him as he galloped toward the bluff. As Fargo fired, Reese's broad-brimmed black hat suddenly flew from his head.

Fargo grinned bleakly as Reese reined in and motioned for his companions to do the same. They turned their horses and rode quickly out of range of the handgun. Then they stopped again and Reese turned to glare toward the river.

"Fargo!" Reese bellowed. "You're beat, Fargo! No place left to run!"

Sparks stuck his head up beside Fargo's for a look. "That son of a bitch is right," he said. "We ain't goin' nowhere, Fargo."

Fargo glanced both ways along the bluff. Sparks was correct. They could work their way along the bluff for a short distance in either direction, but then the slope grew steeper and more sheer, and there were no ledges leading along it. Fargo looked down toward the Brazos. They couldn't climb down the bluff, either, and the river was too shallow to jump. No doubt about it—they were pinned down good and proper.

Fargo's mouth quirked with anger. He didn't like admitting defeat any more than Isaac Reese did. In that way, but in no other, the two of them were alike, he supposed.

His glance at the river had shown him the bodies of the horses and the wreckage of the wagon. They could forget about reaching Fort Phantom Hill in time, Fargo told himself bitterly. Those supplies would never even get to the fort now. Reese had won. Fargo knew better than to blame himself—he couldn't have been in two places at once—but even so the outcome galled him.

Washburn had recovered his senses. He moved up alongside Fargo and Sparks and said, "What's Reese yellin' about?"

"Come on up, Fargo!" Reese was shouting. "My boy Bart's dead, and I got a score to settle with you!"

Sparks put a hand on Fargo's arm. "If you go up there, Reese'll kill you. You know that, don't you?"

"I figured at much," Fargo replied dryly.

Washburn snorted. "Hell, he'll kill all of us. He ain't the sort to just let something go. He beat me"—the same sort of bitter defeat that Fargo was experiencing tinged Washburn's voice—"but that won't be enough for him. He'll want to wipe us out, so that other folks will know not to go up against him in the future."

Fargo agreed. If they surrendered to Reese, their lives were forfeit. But if they put up a fight, were they only delaying the inevitable?

"You have any cartridges for that Spencer?" Fargo asked Washburn

"A few in my pocket. That's all."

Fargo nodded. "And I have a few fresh rounds for my Colt."

"I'm plumb out of ammo and something to shoot it with," Sparks volunteered. "My greener was on the wagon."

Fargo looked at the bloodstain on the old man's shirt. "Are you all right?"

"Yeah, one of those buzzards just winged me. Nothing but a scratch. And I twisted my ankle a mite when I landed. By and large, though, I feel pretty fair."

Fargo had to grin at the old-timer. Sparks had the sort of resilient pioneer spirit that had carried thousands of men through trying times here on the frontier. No matter how strong a man's spirit was, though, sooner or later he was liable to run up against odds that his body couldn't overcome. This was shaping up to be one of those times.

Reese had stopped shouting. Fargo thought that he and the others were probably trying to figure out what to do. The situation was trickier than it might appear to be on the surface. If Reese and his men charged, some of them might well be killed in the fight. With nothing but open air and a fall to the river at the backs of the defenders, there was nowhere for Fargo and his companions to go, but likewise, Reese's party couldn't overrun their position. The easiest and probably smartest thing for Reese to do, Fargo realized, was to try to wait them out. While he was doing that and keeping Fargo and the others pinned down, Reese could also split his forces and send men working around them. If Reese could get some riflemen on the far side of the river, picking off Fargo, Washburn, and Sparks would be like aiming at targets in a shooting gallery.

Washburn must have been thinking similar thoughts. He sighed and said, "No two ways about it, boys, we're up the creek without a paddle."

Fargo ventured another glance over the rim. Movement caught his eye. There was a line of trees in the distance, and as he watched, a wagon emerged from the trees and rolled toward the spot where Reese and the others waited. Fargo couldn't make out much about the driver, but the figure was about the right size to be Susannah. Reese had brought along supplies of his own for his gang of killers, and it made sense that Susannah would be in charge of them so that all the men could devote themselves to their deadly quest.

When Susannah saw what was going on, when she found out that her father had achieved his goal of stopping Washburn from reaching Fort Phantom Hill in time, would she step forward and say that that was enough? Would she try to convince Reese that cold-blooded murder was not necessary? Fargo would have liked to think so, but he doubted it. He remembered how Susannah had tried to plunge his own Arkansas toothpick into his back in that hotel room.

But then she had been acting in the heat of the moment, after he'd been caught up in the life-and-death brawl with her brothers. Things might be different now.

Not that it would really matter. Even if Susannah objected to her father's plans, Reese would just overrule her. If she dared to oppose him very much, she could very well get a beating for her trouble. She had to know that.

No, they couldn't look for any help from Susannah, Fargo decided. To think otherwise would be to delude themselves.

"I sure hate to let that bastard get the better of me," Washburn muttered. "He's going to get that government contract now."

"If we could get out of this mess," Sparks said, "we could tell that Major Gilmore what Reese done. Surely the army wouldn't give him a contract if they found out he wrecked your wagon and tried to kill us."

"If we're dead, no one can prove what happened to us," Fargo pointed out. "That's another reason Reese can't afford to let us live. He doesn't want any witnesses talking to the army."

"Who else would've wanted us dead?" Sparks asked.

"Reese could always blame our deaths on the Indians. The Kiowas have been raiding around here. No one would ever be able to prove they weren't the ones who stampeded our horses, wrecked the wagon, and shot us full of holes."

"Yeah, that's the story Reese will tell, all right," Washburn said dully. "The son of a bitch is smart. Evil, but smart."

As if he had heard them talking about him, Reese called out, "Fargo! Washburn! You been thinking about it? Come on up from there!"

"Is that Spencer loaded?" Fargo asked Washburn.

The freighter handed over the rifle. "I'd just put a round in it when you grabbed me and flung me off the wagon."

"Thanks." Fargo thrust the barrel of the Spencer over the rim, sighted quickly, and pulled the trigger. The rifle bucked against his shoulder as the shot cracked. One of Reese's men jerked in the saddle but grabbed the horn and didn't fall. Fargo was sure he had wounded the man. He handed the Spencer back to Washburn.

"I don't reckon we can answer any clearer than that," Fargo said.

"Damn you!" Reese shouted. "Damn you to hell, Fargo!"

With the sun shining brightly on them as it made its way to the west, hell was probably just what the face of this bluff was going to feel like before the day was over, Fargo thought grimly.

# 10

As the sun inched its way directly overhead and then began the long, slow slide down the western half of the big Texas sky, Fargo's mental prediction began to come true. The scrub brush that grew on the limestone face of the bluff didn't offer enough shade to do any good. The temperature rose higher and higher as the sun blasted against the bluff.

Fargo blinked away beads of sweat that trickled into his eyes and stung them. He looked at his two companions. Washburn's normally ruddy face was even more flushed than usual. He was sweating heavily and panting like a dog. Sparks didn't seem to be bothered very much by the heat, however. The leathery old-timer reminded Fargo of a lizard sunning itself on a rock. He was glad that Sparks was with them. The old man had taken it upon himself to keep a constant watch up and down the river, in case some of Reese's men tried to cross the Brazos and get behind them. So far, that hadn't happened. Reese was showing some patience now that he thought everything was going his way.

Sparks said, "I think we ought to try gettin' off this cliff. I think I can climb down to the river."

"There aren't enough places to hang on to," Washburn said. "You'll fall and break every bone in your body."

"That's better'n sittin' here watchin' you sizzle like meat on a spit."

"Me? What about you? Aren't you hot?"

"It's a mite warm," Sparks allowed. "I've seen it hotter, though. I recollect once up in Kansas when it was so hot the prairie dogs shaved themselves, hopin' it'd help 'em cool off."

Washburn snorted. "That never happened!"

"I ain't sayin' it happened. I'm just sayin' I recollect it."

"I remember loadin' sacks of grain in the summer when

I was a kid and worked for a mill up by the Red River," Washburn said. "Lord, Lord, was it ever hot. You'd sweat so much that the dust from that grain would stick to you and coat you all over like a second skin. You had to breathe the stuff all day long, the air was so thick with it. I'd cough up a handful every night. Now *that's* a true story, not some tall tale like prairie dogs shavin' themselves."

"There was another time," Sparks went on, as if he hadn't heard Washburn, "when it was so hot and dry that when a man went to take a leak the stream would dry up before it had a chance to hit the ground. It'd just arch out a little ways and then disappear."

"I can almost believe that one," Washburn said. "Feels like it's almost that hot now. You know, I have this dream sometimes where I can fly like a bird. Wish it was true now, because I'd sure fly away from this cliff."

Sparks grimaced. "What's Reese goin' to do, anyway? Just sit up there and wait for us to fry?"

Fargo nodded solemnly. "That's what I figure."

"Maybe we ought to go up and give him a fight." Sparks gestured toward the knife in Fargo's boot. "If you'd give me the loan of that Arkansas toothpick, Fargo, I'd carve my initials in that son of a bitch's ornery hide."

"You'd never get close enough to do that," Washburn said. "There are too many of them, with too many guns."

"Well, you got a better idea?" challenged Sparks.

A sudden burst of gunfire kept the exchange from developing into an argument. Fargo's head came up in surprise. Something about the shots didn't sound right. Reese and his men weren't just peppering the rim with lead to keep the tension on Fargo and his companions. The shooting was more frantic than that, the shots coming fast, even sounding desperate.

And then Fargo heard something else that changed everything.

*War whoops.*

Washburn and Sparks heard the shrill cries, too. Washburn exclaimed, "What'n blazes?"

Fargo lifted his head and carefully looked over the rim. What he saw didn't really surprise him, given the reports he'd heard over the past few days about Kiowa Indians raiding in this part of the country. Isaac Reese and his companions were under fire from a band of painted savages on horseback. They had taken cover under the wagon that Fargo had spotted earlier, the vehicle he had thought was being driven by Susannah Reese. Puffs of gunsmoke came from under the wagon as the group of seven or eight whites tried to fight off what appeared to be at least two dozen Indians.

Washburn and Sparks had straightened enough to watch the battle, too. Sparks said, "They ain't got no chance. Those redskins'll wipe 'em out."

Fargo's lips drew back from his teeth in a grimace. Sparks was probably right. The defenders were outnumbered three to one and pinned down under the wagon. The tables had definitely turned on Reese.

But Susannah was over there, too, in just as much danger as her father and her brothers and her father's hired guns. Fargo hated to think of the humiliation, torture, and ultimately death that awaited her at the hands of the Kiowas. Susannah would be better off if she was killed outright during the fighting.

The thought of that rubbed Fargo the wrong way, too. Without thinking too much about what he was doing, he raised the Spencer and thrust the barrel over the lip of the bluff.

Washburn's hand caught the rifle barrel and forced it down. "What the hell are you doin'?" he asked. "Those Kiowas may not know we're over here. If we keep our heads down, once they're finished with Reese they'll likely ride away and leave us alone."

"Washburn's right," Sparks put in.

Fargo's bearded jaw tightened, then he lowered the Spencer. His two companions were right. If he took a hand in this fight, he'd be throwing their lives away for no good reason. They couldn't save Reese and the others, no matter what they did.

"All right," Fargo said. "I don't like it, but . . . all right."

He turned and put his back to the bluff for a few minutes as the shooting and whopping continued up above. From here he could look out across the Brazos and the rugged hills beyond. It was beautiful country, no doubt about that, and someday it would make a fine place to live. But to Fargo it was dark and bloody ground, becoming darker and bloodier with each passing moment.

Gradually, the gunfire lessened and eventually died away entirely. Fargo ventured another look, and what he saw made the blood pound wildly in his head.

The Kiowas had Susannah. Fargo could see her long, light brown hair shining in the sunlight as it hung freely around her face. She struggled in the grip of two of the warriors as they dragged her toward a horse.

"Aw, hell," Washburn muttered from beside Fargo. "Now what're we goin' to do?"

"Look at the wagon," Sparks said.

Fargo's gaze shifted to the wagon. Several of the Kiowas still had their rifles trained on it, as if it represented some threat. Were some of the men still alive under there?

The Indians who had hold of Susannah threw her over the back of the horse. One of the men vaulted up behind her to hold her there. The other warriors mounted their ponies, including those who were covering the wagon with their rifles. Then, with whoops and shouts of triumph, the entire band rode off, taking Susannah with them as their prisoner.

No one emerged from under the wagon. Fargo, Washburn, and Sparks waited tensely for the Kiowa war party to disappear from view. When they were out of sight, Fargo grated, "Come on," and scrambled up over the rim of the bluff.

He ran cautiously toward Reese's wagon, in case anyone was still alive under there and might decide to take a shot at him. Washburn and Sparks followed.

As Fargo drew closer to the wagon, he heard a feeble voice calling for help. Still wary of a trap or trick of some kind, Fargo kept the Spencer trained on the wagon as he approached. He saw bodies sprawled underneath the vehicle. Not all the men were dead, however. Isaac Reese came crawling out from the carnage.

Reese was hatless and his white hair was in disarray and streaked with crimson stains. His clothes were bloody, too. His voice shook a little as he said, "Fargo? Help us, Fargo."

A part of Fargo wanted to ask why the hell he should do that, but it was only a small part. The rest of him couldn't turn his back on someone in need. He went over to Reese, shifted the Spencer to his left hand, and used his right to help Reese struggle into a sitting position with his back propped against one of the wagon wheels.

Reese's breath rasped in and out of his wounded body. "Those damned Indians . . . took Susannah."

"We saw them ride off with her," Fargo said coldly. "Why didn't they kill you, Reese?"

"Reckon they thought . . . I was as good as dead . . . already. They knew I was . . . shot up bad."

"Hey!" Sparks said as he crouched to look underneath the wagon. "There's another one alive under here!"

Washburn gave him a hand, and they pulled Malachi Reese out into the sunlight. Malachi's clothes were blood-stained, too, and he had a nasty welt on his face where a bullet had grazed him. He was stunned, seemingly unaware of where he was or what had happened to him.

"Where's Lucius?" Reese asked. "Where's my other boy?" His voice was a bit stronger now. His wounds might be serious, but Fargo decided that Reese wasn't on the verge of death.

Fargo checked under the wagon, saw Lucius Reese lying on his side with his head in a pool of blood. A bullet had ripped out his throat and severed his jugular vein. His eyes were open wide, staring sightlessly.

"Lucius is dead, Reese," Fargo said. "But Malachi's alive and doesn't appear to be hurt too bad."

Reese closed his eyes for a moment and murmured, "Lucius." The man was an evil, ruthless bastard, Fargo thought, but he wasn't totally without human feelings and emotions. Then Reese opened his eyes and looked up at Fargo and said, "You got to go get her back from those savages. You got to, Fargo."

"Susannah," Fargo said flatly.

Reese's bloody head jerked in a nod. "She's my little girl, Fargo. You got to save her. Malachi and me, we're too shot up to go after them. But you could do it."

Washburn said harshly, "Why the hell should we care? You tried to kill us over and over, you wrecked my wagon, and ruined my chances of gettin' that freight contract. Damn you, Reese, why should we care?"

Reese stared up at him without speaking for a moment,

then abruptly laughed. "You're right, Washburn. That's just the way I'd feel if the boot was on the other foot."

A look of horror and disgust came over Washburn's face. "Ah, damn it!" he burst out. "Why'd you have to go and say *that*?"

Fargo had already made up his mind before the exchange between Washburn and Reese. The Ovaro was around here somewhere. He was going to find the stallion and then set out on the trail of the Kiowas who had carried off Susannah. It didn't matter what she had done in the past. She needed his help now. As for Washburn and Sparks, they would have to make up their own minds.

"I'm going after her, Reese," Fargo said. "I can't make any promises, but I'll do what I can for her."

"Yeah, I reckon I'm in, too, if I can find a horse to ride," Washburn grumbled.

Reese said, "The redskins ran off all our horses, but if you can round up one of them, you're welcome to him, Washburn."

"Better round up two," Sparks put in. "I'm goin', too. Got nothin' better to do right now."

"And you love a good fight, don't you?" Washburn said.

Sparks's lined face creased even more in a grin. "Reckon I do."

There would be a fight, Fargo thought. Unless they were extraordinarily lucky, they wouldn't be able to get Susannah Reese away from the Kiowas without one. But as to whether or not it would be a good one . . .

That was a whole other question.

A check of the rest of the men in Reese's party showed that they were all dead. Reese and Malachi were the only survivors. Two of the dead were the men Fargo had fought with in O'Bar, just before he was forced to kill Bart Reese. His face was impassive when he saw their bodies. He regretted any loss of life, but by signing on with Reese, these men must have known that they were risking a violent end. Now it had come to them.

"Mal and I will bury them when we get some of our strength back," Reese said. "Don't waste time on the dead, Fargo. Take out after those Kiowas before they get too big a lead on you."

"They didn't seem to have any idea we were over there under the rim of the bluff," Fargo said. "So they won't be expecting any pursuit. We'll catch up to them, don't worry."

"I just want my little girl back safe and sound," Reese said with a sigh.

Fargo walked into the trees, whistled loudly, and a few moments later, the Ovaro came crashing through the underbrush. The big black-and-white paint seemed to be unharmed. Fargo was glad the stallion had taken off for the tall and uncut when the Kiowas showed up. Such a fine horse would have been too much temptation for the Indians to pass up. They would have tried to catch the Ovaro and might have even succeeded, though Fargo wouldn't have bet money on that.

Once he was mounted, Fargo rode along the bluff until he found a couple of the horses that Reese and his men had been riding. Fargo hazed them back to the wagon. Though nowhere near the animal that the Ovaro was, the horses would do as saddle mounts for Washburn and Sparks.

"We're taking some supplies from your wagon, Reese," Fargo told the man. "All of ours went over the cliff and into the river with our wagon."

Reese waved a hand. "Take whatever you need. Nothing matters except getting Susannah back."

Fargo packed enough food for several days in the saddlebags of the Ovaro and the two horses that Washburn and Sparks would ride. Even though the Kiowas wouldn't be expecting any immediate pursuit, they wouldn't linger very long in an area where they had been raiding, either. Though Fort Phantom Hill was undermanned at the moment, a cavalry patrol might be sent out after the Indians if word reached the fort of their depredations.

Fargo tended to one other chore before he was ready to ride. His hat had come off when he threw himself and Washburn out of the wagon just before it crashed. He found the hat on the rim of the bluff, picked it up, slapped it against his leg to get the dust off, and pushed the crown back into its usual shape. Then he settled it on his head, ignoring the way it made the bullet crease from a couple of days earlier twinge for a second. He just felt better with his hat on.

He took hold of the Ovaro's reins, said, "Let's go," and swung up into the saddle. Washburn and Sparks followed suit. They had armed themselves with Colts and Henry rifles and a shotgun from among the dead in Reese's party, and they had plenty of spare ammunition. The three men were a small but dangerous group as they set out after the Kiowas.

The Indians had headed northwest, following the eastern bank of the river. Fargo knew that the usual stomping ground of the Kiowas was far to the north in the Texas Panhandle, around the Canadian River, but like their equally warlike cousins, the Comanches and the Kiowa Apaches, they raided wherever and whenever the spirit moved them. Less than fifteen years earlier, a huge band of the combined tribes had gone on a rampage that had taken them all the way across Texas to the Gulf of Mexico, burning and looting and killing along the way. No raids of that scale had been attempted since, probably because of the straggling line of frontier forts that the army was building in Texas, but no one had been able to figure out how to keep the smaller bands of marauders from slipping through and wreaking bloody havoc from time to time.

Fargo had no trouble following the trail of the Kiowas. They weren't trying to conceal it. The unshod hooves of their ponies left plenty of tracks. After riding for miles, in the late afternoon Fargo and his companions came to a place where the bluff alongside the river sloped down gradually enough for the horses to negotiate it. That was where the Kiowas had crossed the Brazos. Fargo, Washburn, and Sparks did likewise and picked up the trail on the far side of the river in the fading light.

"Can you read sign at night, Fargo?" Washburn asked.

"Not well enough to risk it, not without a full moon and plenty of stars." Fargo nodded toward some clouds on the northern horizon. "And I don't think we're going to have that."

Washburn frowned. "If it comes a rain, that'll wash out the tracks."

"I know," Fargo said with a solemn nod. "That'll make our job harder. But I won't give up."

Sparks chuckled. "I didn't much figure you would."

The clouds moved in with the dusk, but the thickest part

of them seemed to be sliding past to the northeast. As they made a cold camp, they saw lightning flickering in the distance, too far away for the accompanying thunder to be heard. A few large, widely scattered raindrops fell, smacking into the dusty ground with a sound almost like gunshots, but that was all. The storm moved on to the east.

The three men made a meager supper of jerky and stale corn bread, then tried to get some sleep. Fargo was all too aware that Susannah Reese might be suffering the tortures of the damned at this very moment. But it was also possible that the Kiowas might decide to just keep her prisoner and postpone their brutal sport with her until they reached their own hunting grounds. Fargo was going to cling to that slender hope. He finally dozed off.

They were up early the next morning and on the trail again. The brief flurry of rain the night before hadn't been enough to wipe out the tracks. From time to time Fargo checked the droppings left behind by the Indian ponies. They told him that the Kiowas were continuing to move at a fast pace today, but they weren't quite as far ahead as they had been when the chase started the day before.

As they rode along, Sparks asked, "What do you figure on doin' when we catch up to them red devils, Fargo, since there's only three of us and more'n two dozen of them?"

"We can't take them on in a battle," Fargo said. "Two many of them have repeaters that they've stolen in their raids. Down south of here, at Bandera Pass, Captain Jack Hays and a few of his Rangers stood off hundreds of Indians back in the forties, but Hays and his men had Paterson Colts while the Indians were armed with bows and arrows. When the Comanches and Kiowas started getting hold of rifles, it changed everything."

Washburn grunted. "Not all of those rifles are stolen. I've heard rumors that somebody's been sellin' guns to the Indians for the past couple of years."

"Some fellas will do most anything for money," Sparks said with a shake of his head.

Fargo didn't doubt that. Nor did he doubt that some unscrupulous men were supplying the Indians with rifles. It was an old story on the frontier.

They left the hills behind. As the land flattened out and became more arid, the vegetation changed as well, becoming more sparse. Some of the oak trees gave way to mesquites. Cottonwoods still grew along the creeks, but they were smaller here than they were down in the Cross Timbers area. The grass was not as lush, and it was beginning to turn brown in places with the advance of summer. In the distance, an occasional mesa jutted up from the prairie.

"This sure is a big, empty country," Sparks commented. "Kind of ugly, too."

They were following a narrow stream. Washburn gestured toward it and said, "That ain't still part of the Brazos, is it?"

Fargo nodded. "I think so. The river split into two main branches, back there a ways behind us, but those branches split up even more. I've heard this called the Seven Fingers country, because there are supposed to be seven fingers of the Brazos. I figure this one we're following is the one called the Double Mountain branch. I rode through here on my way to the Panhandle a few years ago."

"Is there any place in the West you ain't been?" Sparks asked.

Fargo grinned. "Bound to be," he said. "There's not time enough in any one man's life to go everywhere. I reckon I'll give it a try as long as I last, though."

By nightfall, Fargo estimated that they were less than an hour behind the band of Kiowas. All day long, every time he had spotted some strange shape on the ground, he had felt a moment of dread, thinking that as they rode up on it they might discover it to be Susannah's mutilated body. Each time, however, that had proved not to be the case. It was always a cluster of rocks or a fallen tree or some such. The fact that they hadn't found her body was pretty strong evidence that she was still alive. The Kiowas wouldn't have bothered dragging the corpse of a white woman with them. The Kiowas, along with the other Plains Indians, regarded themselves as the only true human beings. A dead paleface was less than nothing to them.

"Early tomorrow morning, before dawn, I'm going to see if I can slip up on their camp," Fargo said as they ate their supper that evening. "We'll stand our best chance of getting away if one of us can get into the camp and sneak Susannah out of there without them knowing. Then we'll ride like hell."

"Might work," Washburn said. "Our horses are probably a mite fresher than theirs."

Sparks nodded in agreement. "Most of 'em will be sound asleep early in the mornin' like that."

"That's what I'm counting on," Fargo said.

Now that the pursuit was nearly over and he was facing the prospect of action again, he had no trouble sleeping that night. He woke early, his internal alarm rousing him while the stars still glittered brightly overhead and there was not even a hint of gray in the eastern sky. He traded his boots for moccasins that he took from his saddlebags, then woke Washburn and Sparks.

"Be ready to ride as soon as I get back," he told them. "We'll probably be leaving in a hurry."

"Are you going to get a horse for the girl?" Washburn asked.

"If I can. If not, my Ovaro can carry both of us. But that'll slow us down, so I want to avoid it if possible. Still, the main thing is getting Susannah out of that camp alive and in one piece."

He left the stallion with Washburn and Sparks and started out on foot, moving in an easy, ground-eating lope. The Apaches could run all day like that, and Fargo had learned from them. It was so dark that he couldn't see the tracks left by the Indian ponies, but he kept moving in the same general direction that they had been going for the past two days, steering by the stars.

He came to a long, gentle rise and started up it, slowing before he reached the top. There was a faint hint of wood-smoke in the air, as if a fire had been burning near here some time earlier. After a few more moments, he took off his hat and dropped to his hands and knees, crawling forward in the short grass. By the time he reached the crest of the rise, he was on his belly.

Now Fargo smelled horses and unwashed human flesh. He edged up a little more, his keen eyes peering as intently through the darkness as they could. The ground fell away more steeply on the far side of the rise, dropping into a broad shallow swale. This was a buffalo wallow, Fargo realized, a depression hollowed out of the prairie by the rolling of countless shaggy bodies belonging to the vast herds of buffalo that migrated through here every year. Farther north on the Great Plains, there were even more buffalo, herds so large that they numbered in the millions, but northern Texas had quite a few of the shaggy beasts, too.

What was most important right now was that this buffalo wallow was serving as a campsite for the Kiowa war party. Fargo saw the dark, bulky mass of their ponies to his right. The warriors were sleeping on the ground, rolled in buffalo robes. Fargo didn't see any Indians standing guard. They considered themselves completely safe out here, far from the advancing line of the white man's civilization.

Fargo's eyes narrowed to slits. Which of those dark shapes on the ground was that of Susannah Reese? He listened, concentrating on the sounds of the night, and after a moment he heard a faint whimper. Fargo waited. A few minutes later, the sound came again, and this time he was able to get a better fix on where it came from. Even though she was probably sleeping from exhaustion, Susannah was still making small whimpering noises, her slumber haunted by nightmares bred by her captivity. Fargo felt certain of that. Again he heard the whimper, and now he was sure from where it originated. He slid over the crest of the rise and started crawling on his belly toward Susannah.

Where she was lying, she was flanked by two of the Kiowas. She could have reached out and touched either of them. Getting her away from them was going to require absolute quiet, Fargo knew. He couldn't afford to make even the smallest sound. Nor could he allow Susannah to cause any noise. That would be even more difficult. He had confidence in his own ability to move silently, but not in hers.

Inch by inch he slid forward, sometimes stopping and freezing motionless for long minutes to make sure that none of the Indians had been alerted somehow to his presence. The ponies shifted restlessly, and Fargo froze again. He didn't know if they had caught his scent and been spooked by it, or if they were just moving around. After a moment they settled down again.

Barely breathing, Fargo continued slipping closer and closer to Susannah. He lifted himself on hands and knees. He had to crawl *over* her, so that he could drop his weight on her and keep her from moving around when he woke her. At the same time, his hand would clamp over her mouth to prevent any outcry. Once she was awake and knew who he was, then they would have to crawl out of here, still without disturbing any of the Indians sleeping so close by.

Any reasonable man would have thought it was impossible. But there were times, Fargo knew, when it didn't pay to think about what was reasonable.

He poised himself above Susannah's sleeping form, ready to try to wake her in utter silence.

That was when the footstep suddenly sounded close behind him, and fingers tangled in his thick black hair, jerking his head back vigorously.

# 11

Fargo knew what was coming next. With his head pulled back like that and his neck stretched taut, the razor-sharp blade of a knife would sweep across his throat and open it so that his life's blood fountained out.

Unless he stopped it *now*!

Acting with the speed of thought, Fargo kicked out behind him and at the same time threw himself forward, barely feeling the pain as some hair was yanked out of his scalp. His foot hit something, probably his attacker's shin. Cold steel raked along the side of his neck, slicing a painful gash, but the killing stroke had missed.

Even so, Fargo knew that the life remaining to him might be measured in seconds. He landed on Susannah, jolting her out of her uneasy slumber and causing her to scream and thrash around. Fargo rolled off her and tried to lunge to his feet. Someone tackled him as he did so, slamming him back to the ground.

Fargo thrust up his right hand, felt it impact against someone's face. His fingers hooked blindly, searching for his opponent's eyes. While he was doing that, he also threw his left hand into the air, knowing that the Kiowa warrior might be trying to stab him, since cutting his throat hadn't been successful. Fargo's forearm clashed with the Indian's arm, blocking the downward thrust of the knife. Fargo's hand slid along the man's arm until he seized his wrist.

The Indian's other hand locked on Fargo's throat. Fargo had been able to gulp down some air, so he wasn't going to pass out immediately from lack of breath. But even though he tensed the muscles in his neck as much as possible, the Indian's strength was great. Fargo knew that in a matter of moments, the Kiowa was going to crush his throat.

Fargo brought up his knee. He missed the Indian's groin, but he felt his knee dig into the man's belly. That loosened the grip on Fargo's throat, but only slightly. Fargo slammed his right fist into the Indian's face, then struck again and again. The Kiowa's hand slipped completely off Fargo's throat.

Twisting the wrist of the hand holding the knife, Fargo powered himself into a roll that sent his opponent flying off him. All around him, though, the other Indians were on their feet, shouting in anger and confusion. A gun suddenly blasted, the orange flash from the muzzle splitting the night for a second.

Someone shouted, "No!" in the Kiowa tongue, in which Fargo was reasonably fluent. "He is mine to kill!"

Fargo was willing to bet it was the man who had jumped him who issued that order. And it was obeyed instantly as the other warriors stepped back, shadowy, threatening shapes in the darkness.

His voice harsh from being choked, Fargo said urgently, "Susannah, run! Get out of here! I'll keep them busy!" He doubted that she could get away, even if she kept a clear head and did as he told her, but he was willing to sell his life dearly in order to give her that chance.

Instead, still on the ground, she exclaimed in amazement, "Fargo?"

"Damn it! Run!" he snapped. Still she ignored him, and it was too late now, he saw to his bitter disappointment. The Kiowas had formed a ring around them. Neither of them would get away.

For a second, he considered drawing his Colt and putting a bullet through her head. Better to die like that than being forced to endure whatever the Kiowas had in mind for her. And if he killed her, spoiling the plans of the war party, it might anger them enough so that they would open fire on him and bring his own life to a quick conclusion. Fargo's hand closed around the grip of the heavy revolver.

Before he could draw the gun, something struck him on the back of the head. Fargo pitched forward, aware for only a second that Susannah was screaming again.

Then oblivion claimed him.

The sun was shining when Fargo regained consciousness. Waking up was a big enough shock by itself. The fact that it was daylight didn't surprise him nearly as much as the fact that he wasn't dead.

Fargo kept his eyes closed. The glare from the sun penetrated his eyelids and seemed to burn right into his brain. Pain bit tightly into his wrists and ankles when he tried to move his arms and legs. Fargo knew what that meant.

The Kiowas had staked him out.

A shadow moved over him, blocking the sun at least for the moment. Fargo's eyes flickered open. He could see the tall, muscular shape of the man who stood there, his body haloed by the dazzling sun behind him.

"You are awake," the man said in English. "Good."

"Better than . . . being dead," Fargo croaked through dry, cracked lips.

"Perhaps." The Kiowa warrior chuckled. "Perhaps."

Fargo's tongue was already starting to swell from heat and thirst. "The . . . the woman?"

"The one you risked your life to save? She is here. She is unharmed—for now." The Indian turned and made a gesture. A moment later, another shape was shoved alongside him. Fargo had trouble making it out against the sun, but he recognized the voice.

"Fargo?" Susannah's voice was a wail of despair. "Oh God, I'm sorry, Fargo. I never dreamed you'd come after me like this."

The Kiowa warrior gestured again, and Susannah was jerked away. The Indian hunkered next to Fargo, letting the sun shine full in his face again. Fargo squeezed his eyes shut.

"Fargo," the Kiowa repeated. "You are the one known as the Trailsman?"

Fargo managed to nod. The motion made his head pound with pain.

"I have heard you spoken of in the lodges of the People," the Kiowa continued. "It is said you are a brave man and that you love the land almost as much as the People do."

"I'd . . . like to think so," Fargo rasped.

"Your courage I do not doubt, nor your skill. The way you slipped into our camp proved that you possess both of those things. Your wisdom . . . Ah, that is another matter."

"You speak . . . mighty good English."

The Kiowa spat. "The white man's tongue, taught by those who come to the People bearing the white man's lies. We know now never to believe the white man again. Our dead have taught us this."

Fargo hadn't come here to argue politics. He had just wanted to rescue Susannah Reese and take her back to her father. That effort seemed to be doomed to failure.

But he wasn't going to give up. He said, "Cut me loose. Give me a knife."

"You give orders to your captors?"

"I issue a challenge," Fargo said. He ignored the pain in his cracked lips and went on. "You have said I am a brave man. Honor that bravery by allowing me to fight for my life."

He had already figured out that the Indian who was talking to him was the same one who had jumped him when he tried to sneak into the camp and wake Susannah. The same one who had ordered the other braves to stand back and leave Fargo to him. That meant he was at least a war chief of his band, and as such, a proud man. Fargo hoped to appeal to that pride.

After a moment, the Kiowa said, "It is true that I thought Lame Bear had struck you too hard and killed you, despite my words. If you had died, I would be very angry with Lame Bear. But you live, so he is fortunate. I will not have to kill him for defying me."

"You are the chief of this band?"

"I am called Tree That Burns. I lead."

Fargo knew enough of the Indians' customs to know that Tree That Burns must have taken his name from a vision. To the Indians who lived on the Great Plains, any sort of tree was an unusual sight. One that blazed with fire would make a compelling vision to a young warrior on a quest for his name.

"Tree That Burns," Fargo repeated. "It is a good name."

The war chief straightened, once again blocking the sun. Fargo tried not to sigh with relief at the blessed touch of shade.

"Are you alone, Fargo?" Tree That Burns asked.

"I am alone," Fargo answered. It was true, as far as it went. He had left Washburn and Sparks behind when he approached the Kiowa camp.

"You will stay here," Tree That Burns said. "I will think on your words. If you still live tonight, we will see if you will be allowed to fight for your life."

Then he turned and walked away, and the sledgehammer of the sun smashed into Fargo's face again. Quickly, the heat grew almost intolerable. Fargo could feel his skin baking and peeling.

But he had to tolerate it. That was his only chance for life, and Susannah's only chance for life as well.

But it was hot, Lord, it was hot.


Fargo lost consciousness several times as the day dragged on, and each time he felt himself slipping away, he wondered if it would be for the last time. To have lived the life he had, to have survived all the dangers, to have experienced all the joys, only to have it all burned away by that hellish sun . . . He clung to life with all the stubborn strength in his body, and each time the darkness claimed him, he fought his way back out of it.

Once he thought he heard sobbing. Susannah? Was she crying as the Kiowas forced her to watch the sun baking the life out of him? Was she crying for him, or for herself, or for both of them?

Maybe he imagined the whole thing, Fargo thought. Maybe no one would shed a tear at his death.

He came awake and was aware that once again something was blocking the sun's rays. He forced his blistered eyelids up and saw to his shock that a huge buzzard had landed beside him. The carrion bird was leaning over his face, staring down at him with its beady eyes. The hideousness of that moment was beyond anything Fargo had ever experienced. The buzzard's beak suddenly darted at him, ready to rend and tear his flesh.

Fargo shouted, a deep-throated bellow that drew on a source of strength he had no idea was still within him. The buzzard jerked back, startled by the incoherent yell. Fargo snarled and grimaced and roared, "Get away from me, you ugly bastard!"

With an offended screech, the buzzard took wing, wheeling into the sky above Fargo, leaving behind only its stench and the memory of how it had been looking hungrily at him. Fargo thought that grotesque image was probably imprinted permanently on his brain.

This time, there was no sobbing, but he heard laughter coming from the Kiowas. He was certain of that.

More time passed, and Fargo became aware that the heat had lessened somewhat. Was he dreaming again? Had he finally died? Was he feeling the sweet release of death?

No, he realized when he forced his eyes open. The heat wasn't as bad because the sun had slid far down the western sky, causing a red glare that washed over the land like a scene from Hades. But it was still a lot more tolerable than the brassy pounding the sun had given Fargo while it was more directly overhead.

His chest heaved. He had long since given up struggling against his bonds. The strips of rawhide were tied securely to pegs that had been pounded into the hard ground. Fargo's hands and feet were numb, the circulation cut off by the cruelly tight bindings.

This time he didn't lose consciousness. He was still dazed by the torment he had endured, and his thoughts were sluggish. But he stayed awake, and slowly his senses came back to him. The sun had almost set. He had lived through the day. Tree That Burns had promised him that if he survived the hellish heat, he might have a chance to fight for his life. Would the Kiowa warrior keep his word?

Of course, he was in such bad shape right now, Fargo realized, that he would have no chance in a fight with a week-old kitten, let alone a war chief in the prime of his barbaric life.

But he felt a sense of triumph anyway, simply because he had lived through the day.

Night fell with its customary quickness. Fargo was still

burning with heat, but he knew that was because his body had soaked up so much of it during the day. He heard footsteps nearby, and then suddenly a wet cloth touched his forehead. The cool sensation was exquisite and painful at the same time.

"You're alive," Susannah murmured from close behind him. "I can't believe it. You're still alive."

She ran the cloth over his face, blotted it against his lips. Parched beyond belief, Fargo tried to suck some of the moisture from it. The cloth went away, but a moment later, it was replaced by the neck of a water skin. Susannah trickled several drops of water into Fargo's mouth.

"Not too much at first," she said. "You couldn't stand it. Hang on, Fargo. Just hang on."

Drop by drop, bit by bit, she dribbled the life-giving liquid into his mouth, pausing for long minutes after each drink so that his body would have a chance to absorb the water. He began to feel less light-headed, but he was still burning up. Susannah soaked the cloth and draped it over his forehead and eyes and nose. He drank in the blessed coolness, even though it didn't last long each time. The heat coming off his blistered skin dried the cloth within minutes.

Fargo began to drift in and out of consciousness again as Susannah continued caring for him. He had no idea how much time passed. All he knew was that the burning was better now. Sometime during the night, his hands and feet were cut loose from their bonds. Intense pain shot through them as blood began to flow again through the constricted veins and arteries, but Fargo welcomed the agony. It proved that he was still alive.

Susannah helped him to sit up. She gave him jerky to chew on. That made Fargo feel even better. He washed down the jerky with a long swallow from the water skin she placed in his hands. He was still very weak, but some of his strength had returned, and with it had come hope.

Fargo looked around, fully aware of his surroundings for what seemed like the first time in ages.

The Kiowas were sitting around a small campfire made from dried buffalo dung that gave off very little smoke. They were still in the same buffalo wallow where Fargo had found them. He had been staked out on one side of the wallow, several yards from the camp. The ponies were on the far side of the fire, cropping contentedly on the sparse grass.

The Kiowas talked among themselves, grunting with laughter from time to time. They seemed quite pleased with themselves. Not all of them were engaged in conversation, however. A couple of the warriors kept an eye on the prisoners, watching Fargo and Susannah in the faint glow from the fire that barely reached to where they were. One of them, a tall, powerful man with his arms folded across his bare chest, was Tree That Burns. Fargo knew that without being sure how, but he was certain of the warrior's identity.

After a while, Tree That Burns spoke sharply to the other Kiowas. One man stood up and joined the other warrior who was watching Fargo and Susannah. Tree That Burns took that man's place in the circle around the campfire. For long minutes, the members of the war party spoke among themselves. There was no laughter this time. Their voices were low-pitched and solemn. Fargo had a pretty good idea that they were discussing his and Susannah's fate.

Finally, Tree That Burns nodded and stood up again. He came toward Fargo and Susannah. The two guards stepped back, showing deference to their war chief. Tree That Burns stopped in front of the captives.

"We have talked of what you said, Fargo," Tree That Burns declared. "Your challenge is refused. You will not be allowed to fight for your life and that of the woman."

Fargo felt his spirits deflate momentarily. Even in his weakened condition, he had been looking forward to the slim chance that he would have in single combat with one of the Kiowas.

But he gave in to despair only for a second. Then defiance welled up in him, and he asked, "Are the warriors of the People cowards, then?"

The war chief's features were taut in the firelight. "You will not fight for your lives," he said again. "But it has been decided that you will fight for your deaths."

Fargo stared at him for a second, not comprehending, but then understanding dawned. "If I win, they will be quick, with as little pain as possible?"

Tree That Burns nodded. "And if you lose, your dying

will take a long, long time, and your screams will echo far across the prairie."

Susannah's expression was stark when Fargo glanced at her, but she nodded. She understood as well as he did what was going on. The stakes in the fight would not be life and death, but only the manner of death. Still, a quick end was something to be hoped for, considering the alternative.

And there was something in Fargo that would not allow him to give up completely. As long as he and Susannah were still alive, they would have a chance. As much as anything else, he was playing for time.

"If I agree," he said, "when will I defend my honor? I am weak from the torture of the sun."

Tree That Burns smiled faintly. "You have no confidence in your strength, white man?"

Fargo's voice dripped with scorn as he said, "I have always heard that the Kiowas prefer their enemies strong, rather than weak. Would you fight the woman, instead, or break my legs so that I am a cripple? That would ensure your triumph."

For a second, Fargo thought Tree That Burns was going to jerk the knife from the sheath at his waist and kill him then and there. The warrior's face twisted with rage. But Tree That Burns controlled his anger with a visible effort and said, "I have nothing to fear from you, no matter how long you rest. You will have until dawn, then we will settle this thing between us, Fargo."

Fargo nodded. "Dawn."

Tree That Burns turned and stalked back to the fire. When he was gone, Susannah said shakily, "My God, I thought he was going to kill you just then, Fargo."

"So did I."

"Did you have to insult him like that?"

"It was the only way I could get a little time to recuperate," Fargo explained. "It'll be a hard enough fight as is."

"We're both going to die, aren't we?" Susannah's voice was hollow.

"More than likely," Fargo answered honestly, "But I'm not going to give up just yet."

"After all you've been through . . . Where do you get your strength?"

Fargo managed to laugh. "Just stubborn, I reckon."

A few moments of silence went by, then Susannah asked, "How did you know that chief was the one who's going to fight you?"

"He wouldn't allow anybody else to do it. He knows it's between him and me, just like I do."

"You're saying that the two of you are alike?"

"In some ways," Fargo said. "In others, no. But we're close enough so that we understand each other."

"I don't understand anything anymore." Susannah stretched out on the ground. "I'm so tired . . ."

Fargo reached over and rested his hand on her head. "You've been nursing me for a while. You'd better get some sleep."

"I'm not sure I want to sleep. Not if this is going to be my last night on earth."

"What would you rather be doing?" Fargo asked.

She propped herself on her elbows and lifted her head to look at him. "I'd rather be in a nice soft bed somewhere with you on top of me."

Fargo tasted blood on his cracked lips as they curved in a grin. "That sounds pretty good to me, too. I remember that hotel room in Fort Worth . . . Of course, it ended with you trying to put my own knife in my back."

"I'm sorry about that." Susannah glanced down at the ground. "I'm sorry about a lot of things. I just . . . Well, you were fighting with my brothers, and family is family, even when they're no-good bastards . . ."

"Was it true what you told me about your father not sending you there?" Suddenly, it was important for Fargo to know.

She reached over and took hold of one of his hands, grasping it gently because his skin was so sunburned. "I swear it, Fargo. It was all my idea. The first time I ever saw you, I wanted to go to bed with you. I just thought if I could keep you from helping Washburn at the same time . . ."

"It didn't work out that way."

"No. It didn't." After another moment of silence, Susannah went on, "What happened to Washburn and that old man?"

Fargo kept his voice quiet so that the Indians couldn't

overhear. "They're still out there somewhere," he said. "They came with me to try to rescue you."

"They did? My God, why? After everything my father did—"

"Things changed," Fargo said. "We put that fight aside for this one instead."

"My father . . . Was he killed in the attack?"

Fargo shook his head. "He was wounded but alive when we left him. So was your brother Malachi."

"What about Lucius and the others?"

"I'm sorry," Fargo said. "None of them made it."

Susannah tried to contain it, but a tiny sob escaped from her. She wiped her eyes, then said, "I'm glad Washburn wasn't killed. I tried to tell Pa that wrecking the wagon was enough. There didn't have to be any killing."

"Well, the wagon was wrecked, sure enough. Washburn won't be getting to Fort Phantom Hill in time to get that government contract."

"All that doesn't seem so important now, does it?"

Fargo shook his head. "No, it doesn't."

Susannah scooted closer to him and rested a hand on his buckskin-clad thigh. "I'm sorry, Fargo. If I could go back and change everything, I would."

"I wouldn't," he said.

She looked up at him in surprise. "You wouldn't?"

"Not everything." He stroked her hair for a moment, then slid his hand down her back, enjoying the smooth play of muscles under his touch.

"Fargo . . ." she breathed.

Susannah moved even closer and laid her head on his leg. He draped a hand on her hip, feeling its warmth through the taut denim trousers. After a while, her deep, regular breathing told Fargo that despite what she had said earlier, Susannah had fallen asleep.

He smiled and sat there with her and waited for the sun to rise again.

# 12

Fargo dozed a little during the night. Each time he awoke, he took a long swallow from the water skin beside him. The drinks replaced some of the water that had been boiled out of him by the sun the day before. But he was still thirsty and had to force himself not to drink so much that he made himself sick.

Susannah woke not long before dawn. The Kiowas were stirring, too. During the night, two of the warriors had been on guard at all times, switching out every couple of hours. There had been no chance to get away.

As the sun began to peek over the eastern horizon, Tree That Burns walked over to the prisoners. "It is dawn," he announced needlessly. "The time has come, Fargo. Unless you have changed your mind . . . ?"

Fargo grinned. "Not hardly." He put a hand on the ground to steady himself as he started to get up. His muscles betrayed him for an instant as they quivered with weakness. He caught himself before he fell, but not before Tree That Burns noticed what had happened.

The war chief smiled smugly. "Perhaps I *should* fight the woman. She might give me more of a challenge."

"I'll do my best not to disappoint you," Fargo growled. He straightened all the way to his feet, stood upright, and met the gaze of Tree That Burns.

"I believe you, white man," the Kiowa murmured. He held out his hand, and one of the other Indians placed a knife in it, handle first. In the growing light, Fargo recognized the weapon. It was his own Arkansas toothpick.

"You will fight with the blade you know best, as will I," Tree That Burns said. He held out the knife to Fargo.

Fargo took it, enjoying the way his fingers curved so naturally around the handle. He hefted the knife, feeling the perfectly balanced weight. Just holding it made him feel better.

"Fargo," Susannah said. He looked down at her, and she summoned up a smile. "Good luck."

"Thanks. I'll need it."

The other members of the war party formed a ring around Fargo and Tree That Burns. As they faced each other, Fargo said, "If I kill you, how do I know the others will honor our agreement?"

"They would not dare to do otherwise. They know that if they dishonored me, my spirit would return to haunt them the rest of their days."

Fargo considered, then nodded. "Good enough for me."

"You have my word, Fargo. If you defeat me, you will die quickly and painlessly, and the woman will follow you the same way."

"Thank you, Tree That Burns. And you have my word that I will do my best to see that you die first."

A savage smile stretched across the war chief's face. Fargo knew the expression was mirrored on his own face. As he had said the night before, in some ways the two of them were a lot alike . . .

Tree That Burns struck first, darting forward, feinting to the left, then slashing back to the right with the heavy knife in his hand.

Fargo jerked away from the blade. His muscles ached terribly, and every movement pulled at his blistered skin and made his nerves shriek. But his fighting instincts were intact, and if he were to survive this fight, he would have to rely on them to save him. He tried a feint of his own, but Tree That Burns didn't bite on it. Their knives met, sparks flying from the clash of steel.

Fargo danced back, parrying two more blows from Tree That Burns. He knew that the Kiowa war chief had him on the defensive, and he wished there was something he could do to change that.

Suddenly, Fargo stumbled, and Tree That Burns lunged forward. Fargo threw himself to the right and used his left arm to knock the Indian's knife hand up. The blade raked along the left side of Fargo's neck. Fargo twisted and drove his shoulder into the warrior's chest, knocking him back several steps. When Fargo lifted his left hand to his neck, the fingers came away stained with blood.

"Now your wounds match," Tree That Burns grunted.

With all the other suffering he had endured, Fargo hadn't paid much attention to the gash on the right side of his neck. It was crusted over with dried blood and ached dully, but that was nothing compared to what the sun had done to him the day before. The wound on the other side of his neck stung. Fargo ignored it.

He weaved the Arkansas toothpick in front of him in a taunting motion. "Come on, Tree That Burns," he said. "You're not going to try to talk me to death, are you?"

The war chief snarled and launched another attack. The knife blades rang together again and again as Fargo defended himself against the flurry of thrusts and slashes. Tree That Burns pressed him harder and harder, forcing him back. From the corner of his eye, Fargo caught a glimpse of Susannah. She was on her knees, watching the battle intently. Maybe even praying a little, Fargo thought. It wouldn't hurt.

Finally, Tree That Burns came at Fargo so ferociously that when Fargo darted aside from a sweeping downthrust, the Kiowa leader lost his balance. That was the opening Fargo had been waiting for. He caught the war chief's knife wrist and pulled hard, while at the same time kicking at the Indian's left knee. The kick missed, striking Tree That Burns on the lower thigh instead of shattering his kneecap, but combined with the grip Fargo had on his wrist, it was enough to send Tree That Burns spinning hard to the ground.

Fargo tried to follow up his momentary advantage. He twisted the man's arm and at the same time dropped onto his torso, driving his knees into the other's belly. Tree That Burns grunted in pain. Fargo thrust with the Arkansas toothpick, intending to drive the blade under the Kiowa's left arm and into his heart. Tree That Burns spasmed desperately, writhing around so that Fargo's knife sliced across his ribs but didn't penetrate deeply. Still, the wound was enough to cause blood to flow down his side.

He arched his back and threw Fargo off him. Fargo bit

back a cry of pain as he landed heavily on one shoulder. He rolled over and came to his feet. He was shaky again, but so was Tree That Burns as the war chief stood up, too. Fargo saw surprise in the man's eyes. He was putting up a better fight than Tree That Burns had expected.

For a moment, neither man attacked. Fargo was grateful for the respite. His heart was pounding, and he felt as if flames were consuming him. He was pushing himself harder than any man had a right to expect of his body. He didn't know how long he could keep it up. If he collapsed, that would be the end, both for him and for Susannah.

But not a speedy end, not unless he could manage to defeat Tree That Burns . . .

"You fight well, Fargo," the Kiowa said. "Almost as well as a warrior of the People."

"I take that as high praise," Fargo said. They were both stalling now, he thought, taking advantage of a few seconds' rest.

"You should have been born one of us. Your home is the wilderness, under the open sky."

"I can't argue with that."

Tree That Burns panted a little more, then grinned. "I think I will kill you now."

"You're welcome to try," Fargo said.

For a change, though, he didn't wait for Tree That Burns to come to him. He carried the attack to the Kiowa instead, forcing Tree That Burns to parry several blows. Fargo's momentum carried him close enough to the war chief so that he was able to shoot a short, left-handed jab into the face of Tree That Burns. His fist smacked solidly into the Indian's mouth, rocking back his head. Fargo darted the point of the Arkansas toothpick at his opponent's chest. Tree That Burns turned the blade aside at the last instant with his knife. Fargo went with the parry, sliding his knife inside so that it raked across his adversary's upper left arm. More blood flowed. Fargo twisted the knife and chopped at the Kiowa's already wounded left side. Tree That Burns was in an awkward position and couldn't get his knife back around in time to defend himself. He interposed his right arm instead. Fargo's knife sliced into forearm, cutting so deeply that steel grated on bone. Tree That Burns cried out in pain and threw himself backward just in time to avoid a backhand stroke of the Arkansas toothpick that missed his throat by inches.

Tree That Burns had drawn first blood, but Fargo had spilled more of it. The war chief's wounded right arm dangled at his side with blood dripping from it in a near-steady stream. He reached quickly across his body with his left hand to take the knife from his now useless right. His face twisted in a grimace as that movement pained his wounded left side.

With a shout of rage, Tree That Burns lunged at Fargo, whipping the blade back and forth. Fargo had no choice but to give ground under the furious attack. Tree That Burns was fighting out of control now, however, and when he stumbled, throwing himself off balance, Fargo crouched and swept his leg around, knocking the Kiowa's feet out from under him. Tree That Burns hit the ground hard. The knife slipped out of his left hand. A shout of surprise and dismay went up from the watching warriors.

Fargo pounced, drawing on the last of his strength and speed to throw himself on Tree That Burns. His left hand locked itself around the war chief's throat, while his right pressed the tip of the Arkansas toothpick against the Indian's chest. One hard shove would send the blade between the ribs and into the heart.

Fargo leaned close over Tree That Burns. He grated, "How about a new deal? Your life for ours?" He relaxed his grip on his enemy's throat so that Tree That Burns could answer, but not enough so that he could tear free.

"No!" Tree That Burns croaked. "Kill me, Fargo, and then . . . my warriors will give you and the woman . . . the deaths you have earned."

"Wouldn't you rather live to fight more white men?"

"We made . . . a bargain. Kill me!"

Nervously, Susannah said, "F—Fargo . . . ?"

He glanced up and saw that several of the Indians had their rifles trained on him. Another one had stepped up behind Susannah and grabbed her hair. He had a knife in his other hand, ready to slash her throat.

Fargo looked down at Tree That Burns. "Your life," he prodded. "All you have to do is let us go."

"You . . . dishonor me! Kill—"

Fargo squeezed his throat, cutting off what Tree That Burns was trying to say. He didn't know if the war chief was about to demand once more than Fargo end his life, or if Tree That Burns was going to order his men to kill the two captives anyway. Neither option was what Fargo wanted.

Suddenly, shots blasted out, shattering the calm of the early morning air. The horses neighed wildly and started plunging around. A man whooped and shouted as more gunshots sounded. The Indian ponies broke out of their bunch, stampeding across the fire toward the group of warriors and the two prisoners.

Fargo wasn't sure what was going on, but he was going to take advantage of the distraction. He reversed the knife and slammed the butt of the handle against the war chief's temple. Stunned, Tree That Burns went limp underneath Fargo.

Susannah screamed. The Kiowa who had hold of her jerked her head back, and the knife in his other hand flashed toward her throat. Before the steel touched her, one of the stampeding ponies crashed into the warrior with its shoulder, knocking the man off his feet. He lost his grip on Susannah's hair.

"Run, Susannah!" Fargo shouted. "Get out of here!"

He heard the crack of a gun and saw one of the Indians go down, blood bubbling from a bullet-torn throat. Another warrior was knocked off his feet by a bullet slamming into his chest. Fargo came to his feet and hauled Tree That Burns up with him. He bent at the knees and let the senseless Kiowa fall forward across his left shoulder.

Fargo staggered under the weight as he straightened, but he kept his feet. Horses dashed around him. The members of the war party were busy trying to either catch the ponies or keep from being trampled by them. Fargo had a pretty good idea that Washburn and Sparks were responsible for this confusion. He didn't know if it would do any good in the long run, but at least his two friends had given him and Susannah a chance.

A familiar black-and-white shape loomed up beside him. Fargo felt like whooping for joy. He flung the limp form of Tree That Burns over the Ovaro's back in front of the saddle, then grabbed the horn and swung up onto the stal-

**123**

lion. He saw Paul Washburn a few feet away, riding one of the horses they had brought with them. Susannah was mounted behind Washburn, her arms around his ample midsection, hanging on for dear life as he emptied the Colt in his hand into the chaos around them.

Sparks's greener boomed nearby. The roar made the remaining ponies even more frantic. They scattered out across the prairie, galloping for all they were worth. Fargo, Susannah, Washburn, and Sparks rode after them, leaving the Kiowas behind in the choking cloud of dust kicked up by the terrified ponies. Rifles cracked and bullets whined past their heads, but none of the slugs came close enough to worry about.

Fargo's brain struggled to accept the fact that they had gotten away, at least for the moment. He had endured so much in the past twenty-four hours . . . in the last week, actually . . . and it was difficult to grasp this sudden turn of events. But as his thoughts wrapped themselves around what had happened, his head became more clear, and he looked over at Washburn and grinned. "What took you so long?" he shouted over the thunder of hoofbeats.

"Just waitin' for the right time," Washburn called back. "Took us a while to sneak up on that Indian camp. I ain't built for skulkin'!"

Fargo knew that it would take time for the Kiowas to round up the ponies that had scattered across the plains. That would give him and his companions the opportunity to build up a lead. But he had no illusions about it—the war party would come after them, especially since the fugitives had Tree That Burns as their prisoner now, instead of the other way around.

The Kiowa chief was still unconscious. Fargo hoped that his hurried blow hadn't cracked the man's skull. Tree That Burns might be worth something to them as long as he was alive. The idea of taking a hostage didn't appeal much to Fargo, but sometimes you just had to work with what was available.

They pushed the horses as hard as they dared, for as long as they dared. Finally, when the animals had to rest, Fargo slipped down from the saddle and pulled Tree That Burns with him. The Kiowa flopped on the ground, still unconscious. Fargo turned to peer back the way they had come. He was looking for a dust cloud that would indicate the Kiowas were coming after them. He didn't see anything except clear blue sky vaulting over seeming endless plains and gently rolling hills.

The sun was well up now, and the air was growing hot. Washburn sleeved sweat off his forehead and said, "I don't see any sign of 'em."

"Neither do I," Fargo agreed, "but that doesn't mean they're not back there."

Sparks said, "Not even a bunch of redskins can ride across country this dry without raisin' some dust. Them ponies were scattered to hell and gone. They may be most of the day gettin' everybody in the war party mounted again."

"But when they are, they'll be coming after us," Fargo said. "And they won't let anything stop them from catching up to us."

"Reckon they figure they've got a score to settle with us, all right," Washburn said. "What did they do to you, Fargo? You look like you've been roasted over a hot fire."

Fargo chuckled humorlessly. "I feel about that way, too. They had me staked out all day yesterday. The sun did this."

Washburn shook his head and said, "I wish we'd gotten there sooner. We waited a good long while for you to come back, and when we finally decided that something must've happened, it was too late in the day for us to find that camp. We followed your tracks part of the way, then snuck in the rest of the way this mornin'."

"You did fine," Fargo assured him. "The Indians were already distracted by the fight between me and their chief. You made the most of it by stampeding those horses."

"We were mighty surprised to see that you and the gal were both still alive," Sparks put in.

Fargo took Susannah's hand for a moment and squeezed it. She smiled at him, and said, "We were lucky."

A few feet away, Tree That Burns suddenly stirred and let out a groan. Fargo was glad to see the Indian was finally coming to. He hunkered next to Tree That Burns and waited for him to wake up.

The Kiowa's eyes snapped open, and his muscles tensed. Washburn stuck the barrel of a rifle in his face and said,

"Don't try anything, son. I don't want to blow your head off just yet."

"Better listen to him," Fargo advised.

Tree That Burns relaxed a little. He looked around and said, "I would not lie on the ground like an animal."

Fargo stood up and stepped back. "All right," he said. "You can get up."

Tree That Burns climbed slowly to his feet. He winced slightly but gave no other sign that his head had to be pounding fiercely from the blow that had knocked him out. He looked fiercely at Sparks, who had the scatter gun trained on him, at Washburn, who held the rifle ready, at Susannah, who glared at him with hatred in her eyes, and finally at Fargo, who stood there alert but impassive.

"The spirits have smiled on you," he said to Fargo. "You had one foot in the land of death."

"So did you," Fargo pointed out.

"I will go happily and greet you there."

"Not today," Fargo said. "With luck, nobody else dies today."

Tree That Burns frowned. "You do not mean to kill me? I am your enemy."

"You're also the leader of that war party. They'll think twice about attacking us as long as you're with us."

The Kiowa's face grew dark with anger. "You would use me as a shield?" He spat on the ground. "I thought better of you, Fargo."

Fargo restrained the anger he felt spring up inside him. "We do what we have to," he said flatly. "I want to get my friends back to safety. That's more important to me than anything else."

"I tell you this now," Tree That Burns said. "I will do anything I can to see that you and these others die."

Sparks suggested, "Maybe we should just blow you in half right now." He gestured meaningfully with the double barrels of the shotgun.

Tree That Burns spread his arms, as if inviting the old man to go ahead and shoot.

Fargo stepped between them. "That's enough. I said nobody else dies today. Not as long as I have a say in it. Tree That Burns, you'll ride with me. My horse is the strongest. Susannah, you'd better double up with Sparks."

The old man grinned.

126

"Two horses having to carry double will slow us down," Fargo went on. "We can't push them too had, and we'll have to stop to rest them fairly often. But we'll keep moving, and with luck we'll stay ahead of that war party."

"My warriors will never give up," Tree That Burns said. "They will pursue you forever."

"They can pursue all they want," Fargo said. "They've still got to catch us. Mount up. Let's ride."

Fargo kept the party moving steadily all day, ignoring his own fatigue and the pain from his wounds and sunburned skin. He kept a close eye on their back trail as well. It was late afternoon before he thought he saw a faint haze of dust in the air, far, far behind them. Was it from the war party, or from a herd of buffalo moving through the area? Fargo had no way of knowing, but he was going to assume it was a sign of pursuit by the Kiowas.

Their first dash away from the Indian camp had been concerned only with speed. Since resting for the first time, though, Fargo had picked their route more carefully, leading them over stretches of rock wherever he could find them, walking the horses for a mile or more through the shallow waters of whatever branch of the Brazos they were following, and using broken branches to sweep out their tracks wherever he could. Thanks to his efforts, following their trail would not be easy.

But the Kiowas were good trackers, and Fargo was confident they wouldn't lose the trail entirely. His goal was merely to disguise it, to slow their pursuit down as much as possible.

By the time night fell, they were still in the land of broken mesas, but the terrain was not quite so arid now. Fargo called a halt.

"We can't afford to stop all night," he said, "but the horses need a longer rest this time, and so do we. We'll break out some jerky and eat a little. We need to keep our strength up."

"Sounds good to me," Washburn said. "I'll keep an eye on that Indian, Fargo, if you want to get a little shut-eye."

As much as the idea of sleep appealed to him, something else sounded even better to Fargo. "I thought I might soak these burns in the river for a while."

"That'll be good for 'em," Sparks said. "Don't you worry about the redskin. We'll watch him closer'n a hawk."

Tree That Burns stood there, arms folded, his face disdainful. He acted like he hadn't heard any of the comments about him.

Fargo unsaddled the Ovaro while Washburn took the saddles off the other two horses. They wouldn't leave the animals that way for very long, but the horses needed the rest, too. When that was taken care of, Fargo gnawed a piece of jerky, savoring the taste of the tough, dried meat. A part of his mind was still amazed that he was alive. He had almost resigned himself to death at the hands of the Kiowas, one way or another.

Almost . . . but not quite.

Tree That Burns refused to eat. Fargo didn't press the issue. If the Kiowa got hungry enough, he would eat. In the meantime, having him weak from his stubborn refusal to take any sustenance wasn't a bad thing. It would make him easier to deal with as a prisoner.

When Fargo was finished with the meager meal, he stood up and walked over to the river. It was narrow and shallow along here, too shallow for him to do more than splash handfuls of water on himself. He called over to the others, "I'm going to see if I can find a deeper spot."

Washburn was sitting with the Henry leveled at Tree That Burns. On the other side of the war chief, Sparks had him covered with the greener. "Don't worry about us," Washburn said.

Fargo walked along the river, following it easily in the starlight. The moon had not yet risen. When it did, it would be time to move on and put more distance between themselves and the Kiowas.

Fargo followed the river around several bends, so he was out of sight of the camp when he came to a spot where the stream widened a little, forming a pool. He took off his boots and peeled off his buckskins, grimacing when the clothing dragged over the sunburned skin of his hands and face. He waded out into the water, feeling his toes dig into the sandy bottom. When the water reached the middle of his thighs, he sank down into it and plunged his head under the surface, keeping it there as long as the deep breath he had taken lasted. When he sat up, the cool night breeze blowing against his wet face felt wonderful.

An unexpected footstep made him tense and look around, then he relaxed as he recognized the slender shape moving along the riverbank.

"I thought you might like some company," Susannah Reese said.

# 13

Without waiting for Fargo to reply, Susannah's fingers went to the buttons of her shirt and began to unfasten them. When she spread the shirt open, revealing her bare breasts, Fargo could make out the dark pink circles that were her nipples, standing out against the pale, creamy flesh around them. Susannah took the shirt off and draped it over a small bush on the river bank. She sat down to take off her boots.

"The water feels nice," Fargo told her. "Come on in."

"That's just what I intend to do." She tossed her boots and socks aside, then stood up to unfasten her denim trousers and peel them down over her thighs and calves. She draped them over the bush with her shirt, half turning so that Fargo had a good view of her smooth back and the sensuously rounded curves of her backside. When she turned back to face him, he saw the dark triangle of the tuft of hair between her legs.

Fargo stayed where he was as Susannah waded out into the river toward him. When she came up to him, his face was on the same level as her hips. She moved closer, spreading her thighs a little. Fargo reached up and around to cup the firm globes of her rump and urge her toward him. He buried his face in the thicket of fine-spun brown hair.

Susannah sighed and spread her thighs even more,

crouching a little so that Fargo could move his head between her legs. His fingers caressed and kneaded while his tongue flicked out and darted against the sensitive little bud at the top of her crevice. Susannah gave a muffled cry of passion as his tongue toyed with her.

He parted the fleshy, feminine folds and stroked his tongue up and down, savoring the dew that formed on them. Susannah clutched his head and ran her fingers through his thick dark hair. Her breathing was rapid, signifying the feelings that were building up inside her.

Under the water, Fargo's organ was rigid. His exhaustion and the injuries he had suffered faded away to nothing in the face of his need for Susannah.

He tongued her womanhood for long minutes until his face was soaked with her juices. Her hips jerked as he brought her to her first climax. When it was finished, she gave a long sigh and sank down, straddling him in the water. It would have been easy enough at that point for her to impale herself on his shaft, but that wasn't what she wanted. Not yet.

"Slide over onto the riverbank," she whispered to him. "I've got something for you."

Fargo didn't know how much pleasuring he could stand, but he did as she said, settling on the soft sand of the bank with his member jutting up stiffly and the water coming only to his knees.

Susannah knelt between his legs, half in and half out of the water. She bent over, her long, light brown hair falling around her face and over his groin as well. The sensation as the strands tickled his erect manhood was exquisite—and maddening.

Susannah used her tongue to tease the little opening in the crown of his shaft. She wrapped one hand as far as it would go around the thick, fleshy pole to steady it as she began a series of soft, darting kisses. She rained the kisses all the way down the length of his shaft to the heavy twin orbs at his base. She kissed them as well, then started back up.

Fargo bit back a groan as Susannah opened her lips wide and took the head of his shaft into her mouth. She sucked on it gently as her tongue circled it, coating it with moisture.

The sweet torment went on for several minutes. Fargo lay back, closed his eyes and gave himself over to the sensations coursing through him. When he couldn't stand it any more, he took hold of her shoulders and urged her up over him. She poised there, straddling his hips, and slowly lowered herself onto the shaft that stood up as strong and hard and unyielding as a railroad spike. She made a little sound deep in her throat as he entered her, her soft walls spreading around him. She was so excited and ready for him that he slipped into her with no trouble at all, and in a heartbeat the tip of his shaft was butting up against her very core.

Susannah's hips pumped back and forth as Fargo thrust into her. He reached up and filled his palms with her firm breasts, cupping them and lifting them. Her nipples were hard, pebbled buds of flesh. Fargo stroked them with his thumbs. His caresses made her hips pump with a frenzied desire.

Susannah began to pant breathlessly as Fargo thrust in and out of her. Both of them had been through so much pain and terror that the intimacy they shared now and the pleasure that flowed so freely between them was like balm poured on a wound.

Then, as he drove himself as deeply inside her as he could and began to erupt, they reached their culmination together. The mutual explosion shook both of them. They held on tightly to each other, as if fearing that without that grip, they would go spinning right off the earth and into space.

Fargo filled Susannah, then slumped back against the sandy river bank. She collapsed atop him, falling forward so that her face was next to his. Both of them were covered with a fine sheen of sweat. Susannah's breasts were crushed against Fargo's chest, and he could feel her heart hammering beneath them. His own pulse was pounding, almost with the same rhythm.

Fargo wasn't sure how much time had passed when he sat up with his arms wrapped around her and rolled both of them into the water. After their exertions, the coolness of the Brazos was refreshing. Their heads went under, then broke the surface as they came up. Susannah laughed and shook her head, the strands of wet hair flying around her face. Fargo thought she was beautiful in the starlight.

She sat on his lap, and he cradled her in his arms. They kissed, softly and tenderly. Susannah said, "You should have gotten some rest, Skye, instead of fooling around with me."

"Fooling around with you made me feel better than anything else could have," Fargo assured her. "Though when we get back to civilization, I wouldn't mind sleeping for about a week."

She laughed. "I'd like to keep you in bed for a week, too, but I'm not sure how much sleep you'd get."

Fargo thought that sounded like a mighty fine idea and told her so. They sat there in the water for several more minutes, letting the flow of the river wash away the sweat and the dust, the aches and the pains. Then, reluctantly, they climbed out and started to get dressed.

"I suppose we'll need to get moving again," Susannah said. "The moon will be up soon."

Fargo nodded as he slipped on his buckskin shirt. "Yes, since all we have to do is follow the river, there'll be plenty of light for—"

He stopped short as the boom of a shotgun suddenly filled the night.

Instantly, Fargo broke into a run. Sparks wouldn't have fired the greener unless something was badly wrong. Sound traveled a long way out here on the prairie at night, and the shotgun's report would tell the pursuing Kiowas that they were on the right trail. But it couldn't be helped now. Fargo knew all he could do was try to minimize the damage.

There hadn't been another shot since the first one. Instead of following the river, Fargo cut across country, charging up a small hill and then down the far side into the camp. He saw two figures thrashing around on the ground, evidently locked in a struggle to the death. Not far off, a dark shape lay sprawled on the dirt, not moving.

Whoever that was, he would have to wait. Fargo knew that one of the struggling figures had to be Tree That Burns. Washburn and Sparks wouldn't have any reason to be fighting with each other.

Fargo slowed down as he approached the combatants. The moon was just rising over the eastern horizon. The two men on the ground rolled over again and then stopped, as if one of them had gained the upper hand. Fargo could tell now that the torso of the man on top was bare, and the low, slanting beams of moonlight suddenly revealed a rock clutched in his hand.

Fargo launched himself forward in a dive before Tree That Burns could bring that rock down in a skull-crushing blow. He crashed into the Kiowa war chief. The flying tackle knocked Tree That Burns off the man with whom he had been struggling. Both he and Fargo went rolling over on the ground.

Energized by his passionate encounter with Susannah, Fargo made it to his feet first. He kicked out with a bare foot, his heel striking the wrist of Tree That Burns and sending the rock flying away into the night. With a defiant roar, Tree That Burns surged up from the ground and wrapped his arms around Fargo, trapping the Trailsman in a bear hug. The Kiowa's arms locked around Fargo's torso like iron bands, crushing against his ribs and lungs.

Fargo felt his feet come off the ground as Tree That Burns tried to squeeze the life out of him. With his arms caught in the bear hug and no leverage for his feet and legs, he struck back the only way he could. He lowered his head and drove the top of it into the warrior's face. Tree That Burns grunted in pain as Fargo's head smashed into his nose. His grip eased enough for Fargo to wiggle his right arm free. He brought up the heel of his hand under the other's chin, forcing the war chief's head back. With a cry of anger and frustration, Tree That Burns let go of Fargo and staggered back a step.

Fargo slammed a left into his belly, then sent a right cross rocketing to the Indian's jaw. The combination made Tree That Burns fall to one knee, but he wasn't finished. Not by a long shot. He hurled himself forward, caught Fargo around the knees, and dumped him over backward.

The impact when he landed drove the air from Fargo's lungs. He gasped for breath and threw himself into a roll as Tree That Burns clubbed both hands together and tried to smash them down into Fargo's face. The blow missed and left Tree That Burns hunched over, wide open for a kick into his side. It happened to be his left side, the one

Fargo had gashed deeply during the knife fight in the Kiowa camp, and the blood began to flow again as Fargo's kick reopened the wound.

Tree That Burns scrambled to his feet, as did Fargo. Now, though, the war chief was holding something he had snatched up off the ground. Fargo saw to his shock that it was the scattergun belonging to Sparks. Fargo had heard only one barrel discharge earlier, so that meant the greener still had one unfired shell in it. He tensed himself to dive aside, hoping he could dodge the load of buckshot since it wouldn't have time to spread out much in such a short distance.

Tree That Burns fumbled with the weapon, not being overly familiar with it, and that second's delay made all the difference. Susannah's voice rang out, cold and hard and menacing. "Drop it or I'll shoot!" The metallic ratcheting of a gun being cocked gave added emphasis to her words.

Susannah's voice came from behind and to one side of Fargo. He risked a glance over his shoulder and saw her standing there holding a revolver leveled in both hands. The weapon's barrel was rock-steady and pointed straight at Tree That Burns, who stood with the shotgun's twin barrels still pointing toward the ground. He couldn't hope to raise the greener and fire before Susannah could squeeze the trigger. All he could do was hope that her shot would miss. Fargo hoped the Kiowa would understand that and do the reasonable thing.

Instead, Tree That Burns growled, "I will not be threatened by a woman!"

"Then how about by a man with a sore head?" Washburn asked as he loomed up behind Tree That Burns with the Spencer in his hands. "Put that greener down, damn your ornery hide!"

Tree That Burns hesitated. Glaring at Fargo in the moonlight, he said, "I would willingly join my ancestors now if I knew I could kill you at the same time, Fargo."

"Too bad there's no guarantees in life—or death," Fargo said.

With a snarl of hate, Tree That Burns flung the shotgun to the ground. Fargo darted forward, picked it up, and backed off. They had Tree That Burns covered from three different angles now. If he tried anything, they could blow him to pieces in the blink of an eye, although that was the last thing Fargo really wanted.

"What happened?" he asked tensely.

"Reckon I must've nodded off," Washburn said with disgust in his voice. "Next thing I knew, the redskin had jumped Sparks. Sparks got off a shot, but it went into the air and didn't hurt anything. The redskin knocked him down and then kicked the rifle out of my hands. I tackled him. A minute after that, you came runnin' up."

"Susannah, check on Sparks," Fargo said. "We'll watch Tree That Burns."

She lowered the revolver and slipped the hammer out of its cocked position, rotating the cylinder before she let it down to rest on the single empty chamber. Fargo noted the move with approval. Not surprisingly, Susannah knew what she was doing when she handled a gun.

She went over to Sparks and knelt beside him, lifting his shoulders so that his head rested in her lap. "He's breathing all right," she called to Fargo. "There's a goose egg on his head. Looks like the Kiowa just knocked him out."

"Stay with him until he comes around," Fargo said. To Tree That Burns, he went on, "Looks like we're going to have to tie you up."

"You dishonor me!"

Fargo stared coldly at him. "Right now I don't give a damn about your honor, mister."

Tree That Burns was seething. "Already I bear the shame of being captured by white men and of failing to kill the offspring of my greatest enemy."

Fargo wasn't paying that much attention to the war chief's protests, but those words caught his interest. "Greatest enemy?" he repeated. "What the hell do you mean by that?"

"The white-haired one called Reese." Tree That Burns was practically spitting with hate.

"Wait a minute," Susannah said. "Are you saying that you know my father?"

Fargo was mighty curious about the same thing. He had assumed that when the Kiowa war party jumped Isaac Reese and his bunch while they had Fargo and Washburn and Sparks pinned down, it had been a random attack. The Kiowas had heard the shooting, come to investigate, and

135

taken advantage of the opportunity to wipe out some more of the hated white men. Now, from what Tree That Burns was saying, it began to sound as if the attack had been deliberate.

"I know him," the war chief said. "He has promised much but dealt falsely with me and my people."

Sparks moaned as he started to come around. Susannah helped the old man sit up, then she got to her feet and strode toward Tree That Burns. "That's a lie!" she said, her voice shaking from the depth of what she was feeling. "My father would never have anything to do with a bunch of filthy, stinking murderers like you!"

Fargo was beginning to have a bad feeling about this. "Don't get too close to him, Susannah," he warned. The last thing they needed was for Tree That Burns to grab her and use her as a hostage again. To Tree That Burns, he said, "You'd better explain what you're talking about."

"I am talking about how the white man's promises are always lies," Tree That Burns said haughtily. "The one called Reese lies even more than other white men. He came to us, sold us repeating guns, and promised that he would bring more. He said that soon there would be many goods he could trade with us, not just guns."

"Son of a bitch," Washburn breathed. "*Reese* is the one who's been supplyin' the redskins with guns?"

Fargo's thoughts were racing as he put suppositions together to form a clear picture. "And if he got that freight contract with the army, he could skim off even more ammunition and supplies that he could turn around and sell to the Indians."

"No!" Susannah cried, looking back and forth between Washburn and Fargo. "My father's a . . . a hard, ruthless man. I won't deny that. But he'd never deal with the Indians! Never!"

"Why not?" Fargo asked. "In the time I've known him, it seems like he'd do almost anything for money. Remember how he tried to kill Washburn and Sparks and me, over and over."

"But he wouldn't sell guns to the Indians," Susannah said miserably. "My mother—" She had to stop as a sob escaped from her. "My mother was killed by them, years ago. They . . . they came raiding while my father was gone.

When he came back to the ranch, he found her. They had . . . the things they had done to her . . . scalping her was the least of it—"

Susannah had to stop again as racking sobs shook her. She buried her face in her hands.

"My words are true," Tree That Burns said harshly. "Reese sold the guns to us. But he lied. He told us they were good guns. Some were, but many were not. They did not shoot right. Some did not shoot at all. Many of our warriors went into battle with them and died because the guns did not work. That is why, when one of our scouts saw Reese near the river your people call the Brazos, we came to avenge our dead."

"But you left Reese alive," Fargo pointed out.

"This time," Tree That Burns said, his voice smug. "And we took this girl-child with us. We wished him to suffer the knowledge of what we would do to her. Whether she died quickly or not, Reese would believe that it took many long, painful hours before she was dead." The war chief shrugged his broad shoulders. "Then, another day, we will kill the one called Reese. But death alone is not enough to repay him for what he has done."

To Fargo's ears, everything about the story had the ring of truth. He could believe that Reese would sell guns to the Indians, even though he had lost his wife to an Indian raid years earlier. He could believe that Reese wanted the government freight contract not only for the money he could make from it legitimately, but also for what he could make illegally. The whole thing tied together neatly, whether Susannah wanted to believe it or not.

Sparks had regained consciousness and was on his feet by now. He put an arm around Susannah's shoulders as she cried and said, "Come on, gal. Don't worry about it now."

"He's right, Susannah," Fargo said, as gently as he could. "We'll sort it all out when we get back. Right now we just have to worry about staying alive that long."

She sniffled and wiped the back of her hand across her nose. "I . . . I know. Like you said, you'd better tie him up." She gestured toward Tree That Burns without looking at him.

Fargo took the revolver from her and kept it trained on the war chief's chest while Washburn pulled his arms behind him and lashed them together with strips of rawhide. Being bound like that would make riding more awkward and painful for Tree That Burns, but Fargo couldn't bring himself to summon up much sympathy for the Kiowa.

They mounted up and started south again under the light of the rising moon. Susannah still sniffled from time to time as she rode with Sparks. Fargo thought about the promise he had made to Isaac Reese that he would bring Susannah back safely to him.

Fargo would do his level best to keep that promise. But once he had fulfilled his pledge, there was nothing stopping him from bringing Reese to justice. He thought the army would be mighty interested to hear what Tree That Burns had to say about where the Indians had been getting their repeating rifles.

The night was cooler, and even carrying double, the horses stood up better under those conditions. They were able to ride the rest of the night with only one brief stop. By morning, as the flaming ball of the sun climbed over the eastern horizon, they were back in the edge of the Palo Pinto Hills. The stream they were following had merged with several other branches of the Brazos, and it was a decent-sized river again.

Fort Phantom Hill was off to the southwest somewhere. That was where Fargo intended to go. The horses splashed across the Brazos where some gravel bars made it easy to ford. Fargo took the lead, picking their course by instinct as much as anything else. He thought they could reach the fort in a couple of days, maybe less if all went well.

Leaving the drier terrain had one drawback. If the Kiowas were still somewhere behind them—and Fargo had no reason to believe they were not—their ponies wouldn't kick up nearly as much dust now. They would be able to cut into the lead that Fargo and his companions had established without as much warning. That was why Fargo cautioned Washburn, who was bringing up the rear, to keep a close eye out behind them.

When they paused to rest at midday, Tree That Burns once again refused to eat. He was beginning to look a bit haggard, his face showing the strain of riding all morning with his hands tied behind his back.

"Where are you taking me?" he demanded as the others

chewed on strips of jerky and washed down the dried meat with swigs from canteens filled with river water.

"To Fort Phantom Hill," Fargo replied. "I want you to tell the commanding officer there what you told us about those guns Reese sold to your people."

Susannah had been unusually quiet all morning. She wasn't the talkative type to start with. Today she had said almost nothing, answering with monosyllables the few questions Fargo had asked her. Now, as Fargo mentioned her father, she looked away, an unreadable expression on her face. At least she wasn't crying anymore. Fargo wondered if that was completely a good thing.

When they finished their sparse meal, they mounted up again and rode toward the southwest, following gloomy valleys through the hills. Fargo didn't like the looks of this place. The valleys were too dark, the thickly wooded hills hanging over them like beetling brows. He told himself he was making too much of a simple topographical feature, but he couldn't shake the uneasy feeling he'd had ever since they entered the hills. Out here in this wilderness, a man could find himself feeling that he was traveling through country where nothing human had ever passed before, a land of unknown and unknowable horrors that might at any second well up without warning from ancient depths of the earth . . .

"When we get to the fort," Washburn said, breaking into Fargo's grim reverie, "you reckon they'll have any pie?"

Fargo laughed out loud. "Deep-dish apple pie," he said. "Sounds mighty good."

"I'm partial to peach myself," Sparks put in. "Nothin' better'n a dish o' peach pie with some sweet cream on it."

Tree That Burns made a strangled sound of contempt. "You white men are fools!" he said from the back of the Ovaro where he rode behind Fargo. "Death follows you at every turn of your lives, and you prattle about sweets!"

Fargo glanced over at Susannah. "A man who spends his life fretting about how it's going to end wastes all the good times that come first," he said quietly. "Seems to me that a man who's enjoyed his life doesn't have to worry as much about when it's going to be over."

Tree That Burns just grunted, unable to argue with Fargo's statement.

They rode on, and as they did, clouds rolled in from the west, making the valleys between the hills even darker. The wind picked up, whipping Susannah's hair around.

"Fixin' to come a cloud," Sparks said.

Washburn pointed. "Fixin' to, hell. It's right there!"

Lightning flickered in the sky, and thunder rumbled. As the storm approached, the air seemed to grow charged with some power that craved release. Fargo said, "Maybe we'd better find some place to wait out the storm."

The final words were barely out of his mouth when lightning flashed and a crack of thunder pealed. As it did so, Fargo sensed as much as heard something rip through the air near his head. He twisted in the saddle to look over his shoulder, past Tree That Burns.

A dozen or more riders were boiling up the valley after them, muzzle flashes sparking through the overcast gloom like miniature lightning bolts.

The Kiowa war party had finally caught up to them.

# 14

Fargo drove his heels into the Ovaro's flanks, prodding the big stallion into a gallop. "Come on!" he shouted to his companions. They had to find a place to make a stand.

As all three horses broke into a run, Fargo felt Tree That Burns shift behind him. Thinking that the Kiowa war chief was going to take a chance on leaping from the racing horse, Fargo twisted in the saddle. Sure enough, Tree That Burns was trying to wriggle off the Ovaro's back. With his hands tied like they were, he would probably break his neck if he fell off the horse. Fargo wasn't going to give him that chance.

He reined in sharply, yelling, "Keep going!" to the others. They hesitated anyway until Fargo waved them on with an urgent gesture. Tree That Burns slid to the ground, clearly hoping to make a break for it. Fargo was out of the saddle in a flash. He palmed his Colt and slammed the gun into the side of the war chief's head. Tree That Burns went down, stunned.

With a grunt of effort, Fargo lifted the Kiowa and flung him across the Ovaro's back in front of the saddle, just as he had done before. More bullets whipped past him. The members of the war party weren't being very careful of their chief's safety, Fargo thought. One of those bullets intended for him could just as easily hit Tree That Burns. Fargo's hopes of using the chief as a hostage were evaporating rapidly.

But he could only play the cards as they were dealt. He leaped back into the saddle and sent the stallion pounding after the others. As fat raindrops began to fall around him, he saw they were headed for a small, steep-sided, rocky-topped knoll that backed up to a larger hill. At some time in the past, a fire had burned off much of the timber on the knoll, leaving a considerable number of deadfalls. If they could get to the top of the slope, the fallen trees would give them some shelter from the Indians. It wasn't a perfect spot, Fargo thought, but probably the best they were going to find.

The Ovaro was really stretching out its legs now, running with all its magnificent heart. Fargo reached the bottom of the knoll before the others had made their way to the top. He started up after them. A glance behind him told him that the Kiowas were still a hundred yards away. A bullet ricocheted off a rock beside him, and another thudded into the still-standing trunk of a dead tree.

The stallion had to slow as Fargo guided it through the burned-out skeletons of the oaks that had once covered the knoll. As lightning flashed and crackled again, Fargo wondered if the fire that had denuded this little hill of life had been started by a lightning strike. It seemed likely.

Rain sliced down, slashing at Fargo. The summer heat had vanished. The rain clawed at him like icy fingers. Something struck him on the shoulder. He looked around, saw small chunks of hail bouncing off the ground. The wind howled.

Fargo hoped the storm would slow down the pursuit. When he looked behind him now, the rain was so thick and heavy that he couldn't see more than a few yards. It beat at him like millions of tiny fists, and the hail mixed in with it only made the pounding worse.

He could tell when the slope changed and became more gradual a short distance below the top of the knoll. Washburn shouted, "We're here, Fargo!" Fargo pulled the stallion to a halt and slid down from the saddle, looking around for the others. He spotted them crouched behind fallen logs. They were poking guns back down the hill toward the Kiowas, but no one was shooting yet. Fargo hauled Tree That Burns off the horse and dumped him on the ground, then slid the Henry from its sheath. A slap on the rump sent the stallion on to the crest.

The fierce rain began to slacken as Fargo knelt beside Susannah. Usually, storms this severe moved fast and didn't last too long in any one place. Lighting struck off to the right, so close that the ground shook from the powerful reverberations of the deafening thunder that followed hard on the heels of the flash. Susannah flinched. She wasn't wearing her hat, and her sodden hair was plastered to her head.

Fargo's keen eyes searched for the Kiowas and couldn't find them. Where in blazes had they gone?

Then he saw a muzzle flash and a slug chewed splinters from the log not far from his head. The Indians had gone to ground rather than trying to charge up the slope in the face of the defenders' guns. That was smart. They could work their way up through the deadfalls, staying behind cover most of the time, and close in on their quarry that way.

"Stay down as much as you can," Fargo cautioned Susannah.

"I thought we were going to make it," she said, bitterness in her voice. "I really did."

"Don't give up yet. We can hold them off for a long time up here."

"We're outnumbered four to one, Skye. We can't keep them from getting up here sooner or later."

Fargo couldn't argue that logic with her. He knew she was right. Yet it wasn't in him to give up.

"Maybe we can cut the odds down a little," he said. He rested the Henry's barrel on the log and waited patiently. The rain tapered off even more.

Several minutes later, a shape darted through the mist. The Kiowa warrior was visible for only a couple of heartbeats. Fargo tracked him with the barrel of the Henry and fired just as the Indian was about to dive behind another log. The bullet caught the warrior in midair and flipped him around. He fell short of the log in the limp sprawl of death.

Washburn called over, "That's mighty fine shootin'!"

Fargo levered another cartridge into the Henry's chamber and kept his eyes on the base of the slope. He knew the Indians had seen what had just happened. The death of their comrade would make them even more wary about exposing themselves.

The mist became finer until it stopped completely. As Fargo expected, the downpour hadn't lasted very long. The wind still blew and thunder rolled and lightning put on a brilliant display as fiery fingers raked through the roiling black clouds, but the rain was over for now.

Suddenly, Fargo heard an eerie, high-pitched howl coming from behind them. His head jerked around, and in the slope of the hill that rose behind them, he saw a dark, irregular opening that he hadn't noticed earlier. The heavy rain had masked it. The opening marked the mouth of a cave, Fargo realized. It reminded him of the mouth of a beast, a hungry maw waiting patiently to devour anything unfortunate enough to venture near it. The keening wail was the sound of the wind blowing through the cave and making its way out through small cracks in the limestone hill.

Next to Fargo, Susannah shuddered. "Good Lord! What's that?" Fargo explained it to her, but she didn't look convinced. "It sounds more like some sort of . . . lost spirit or something."

Sparks was crouching close enough to overhear. He cackled and said, "There are some that say what you hear in the caves hereabouts are the ghosts of all the folks who've died in these hills. Could be they'll be hearin' our caterwaulin' soon enough."

Fargo grimaced. He didn't want to hear any talk like that. He hadn't given up. He wasn't going to give up.

Tree That Burns had regained his senses. The war chief said, "Listen to the old one, Fargo. When we kill you, your spirits will be lost forever, doomed to wander these dark hills."

Fargo swung around toward him, bringing the Henry to bear. "Maybe you'd like to show us the way," he snapped, giving in to his anger for a second.

Tree That Burns just glowered back at him, and then Susannah said urgently, "Fargo!"

He whirled around and saw a couple of the Kiowas running up the hill as their companions blazed away with the repeaters, giving them covering fire. Fargo, Susannah, Washburn, and Sparks all had to duck as the fusillade smashed into the logs. When the firing stopped, Fargo knew that the two warriors were closer now to the top of the slope. In a few moments, the war party would probably open up again, and a few more of the Indians would dash farther up the hill. They would work that way, leapfrogging each other, until they were all close enough for a final, concerted rush that would overwhelm the defenders.

Tree That Burns laughed. "You know that you are doomed, Fargo," he said. "I can see it on your face. Soon the buzzards will strip away your flesh and pick at your bones."

At the moment, no one was shooting. Fargo took advantage of the opportunity to raise his voice and shout down the hill, "We have your war chief! Let us go and he will live! Attack us again and he dies!"

There was no response from downslope, and once again Tree That Burns gave an ugly laugh.

"Do any of your men speak English?" Fargo asked him.

"Several speak the white man's tongue well enough to understand you, Fargo. But your threat does you no good, even if you were to carry it out, which I do not believe you would do. The hatred my warriors feel for you is greater than any loyalty they feel for me. And they know that if they spared your lives simply to save mine, I would kill them myself."

Another flurry of shots interrupted the conversation. Once again, bullets slammed into the logs and threw splinters into the air. Recalling that Isaac Reese and his men had pinned him down like this a few days earlier, Fargo thought that he was getting damned tired of hiding behind logs.

Maybe it was time to make some other use of them.

No sooner had the thought struck Fargo than he knew he was on to something. He risked a quick look at the hillside, noting the position of the deadfalls. It might work. He looked around for a sturdy enough branch to use as a lever.

Finding one that might be suitable, he crawled over to it and picked it up. Susannah watched him curiously as he brought the thick, broken limb back with him. He used the Arkansas toothpick to start hollowing out a space underneath the log.

"Skye, what are you doing?" Susannah asked when she couldn't stand the curiosity anymore.

Fargo was finished with the digging. He cleaned the blade and thrust the Toothpick back in its sheath. Wedging one end of the broken branch into the hollow under the log, he placed a rock under it to act as a fulcrum.

"I read something once about an hombre named Archimedes," Fargo said. "He claimed that if you gave him a long enough lever and a good place to stand, he could move the world. I don't want to move the world, just this old tree."

Understanding dawned in Susannah's eyes. "You're going to roll this log down the hill!"

Fargo nodded. "If you can lean on this branch and lift the log even a little, I'll get my shoulder against it and give it a good shove to get it started. When it goes, be ready to jump behind another one for cover, though."

"All right," Susannah agreed. "But this is a big log, Skye. Are we strong enough to do this?"

"You and me and Archimedes," Fargo said with a grin. "Wait until they start shooting again. That'll mean a couple of them are out in the open."

They didn't have long to wait. After a couple of minutes, the Kiowas began to fire. Fargo nodded to Susannah, who threw all her weight and strength against the broken branch that was serving as a lever. The log didn't budge.

Fargo reached over to help her. Finally, the log shifted a little. Instantly, Fargo had his shoulder against it, pushing with all the power he could summon up. Susannah gasped as she struggled to keep the log pried up slightly.

Just when Fargo thought they couldn't do it anymore,

the log shifted even more. It began to roll. "Move!" Fargo shouted to Susannah. He snatched up the Henry and threw himself backward, rolling over another deadfall and dropping behind it. Susannah sprawled beside him.

With a rumble like the thunder that had passed through the area a short time earlier, the log rolled down the hill, slowly at first, then picking up speed. It slammed into several smaller logs and started them rolling, too. The pair of Kiowas who had been dashing up the hill as the rest of the war party covered them glanced up and saw the logs bearing down on them. The two men had time to yell once in surprise and terror before thousands of pounds of dead timber crashed into them and rolled over them, pulping flesh and bone.

Washburn let out a whoop when he saw what Fargo had done. "That's showin' 'em!" he called. "Sparks, let's see if we can't roll one o' these logs down there!"

A few minutes later, the log started by Washburn and Sparks rumbled down the hill. It wasn't as devastating as the one Fargo had launched, but the Kiowas had to duck to avoid it. By that time, Fargo and Susannah were ready again with another log. This one was smaller and bounded down the steep slope, flying through the air and decapitating a warrior who unwisely stuck his head up at just the wrong moment.

The defenders were forced to retreat slowly toward the crest of the hill, giving up their cover as they turned the deadfalls into weapons. The purpose of the maneuver was twofold: The rolling trees discouraged the Kiowas and killed or injured some of them, and it would make the final charge more difficult because the Kiowas would have to attack across open ground.

Fargo dragged the tied-up Tree That Burns the last few feet to the top of the hill as Susannah, Washburn, and Sparks kept up a covering fire. When he was safe, he stretched out behind a rock at the crest of the slope and peppered the Kiowas' position with bullets from the Henry while the others retreated. In a matter of moments, all four of the defenders, plus their prisoner, were ensconced on the very top of the hill.

The overcast sky began to break up, and the sun started to peek through the gaps in the clouds. The temperature rose. The storm had come on them quickly, and now it was moving on just as quickly. Sunshine showered down on the hills, making them not quite so gloomy. The growing heat made steam rise from the wet ground. When Fargo glanced toward the east, where the storm was still moving on, he saw a rainbow arching vividly through the sky. The wind still moaned through the cave behind them, however.

"You reckon we whittled the odds down any?" Sparks asked Fargo.

"I know at least three of them are dead, and I think we wounded a couple more. There's probably about a dozen left who are able to fight."

Sparks chuckled. "Three to one. That's gettin' a mite better."

"And all they can do is rush us," Washburn pointed out. "Since we rolled them trees down the hill, they can't hide behind 'em."

This was almost over, Fargo sensed. The Kiowas would soon lose patience and attack.

They tried a flanking move first, sending a couple of warriors to the right and the left in an attempt to get behind the defenders. Fargo's shot with the Henry brought down one man, and Washburn drilled the other with his Spencer. Washburn grinned and said, "They can do that all day, and we'll just keep whittlin' 'em down."

Fargo didn't think the Indians would risk any more men in the same fashion. They still had the odds on their side, and they wouldn't want to waste that advantage. He glanced at the sun. It was lowering toward the tops of the hills. If the Kiowas waited until it was dark, they ran the risk of their enemies slipping way in the night. So it was simple. They wouldn't wait.

"Get ready," Fargo said quietly.

Tree That Burns began to chant something in his own language, the words coming out in a low, droning, singsong fashion. Sparks exclaimed, "What the hell!"

"It's a death song," Fargo explained. "But I don't think he's chanting it for himself. I think it's his way of telling us that we're about to die. He's trying to make us nervous."

Washburn muttered, "He ain't doin' a half-bad job of it. Reminds me of when ol' Santa Anna had his buglers play their death song for those boys holed up in the Alamo."

Fargo knew the story. None of the Texicans in the Alamo had walked away with their lives. It was going to be different here, today. He swore it.

"Here they come," Susannah said.

She was right. The Kiowas had worked their way up to the last of the remaining cover, and now they broke out from behind the deadfalls, yelling and shooting as they charged forward. Fargo knew that at a moment like this, the most important thing was to keep a cool head, so he tried to ignore the bullets whistling around him as he drew a bead on one of the attacking Indians, squeezed off the shot, then shifted his aim even while the man he had just drilled was falling. He kept shooting, a steady, deliberate fire that cut down several of the Kiowas. Crouched beside him, Susannah fired around the other side of the rock. Beyond her, Washburn and Sparks kept up a steady fire as well. If this was to be the end, Fargo was proud that he was fighting his last fight with such staunch companions.

Sparks was using a rifle, but he dropped it and snatched up his waiting greener as three Kiowas closed in on him. The scattergun boomed and sent one warrior flying backward, his flesh shredded by the charge of buckshot. Another one, wounded, pressed on and leaped over the rock that Sparks was using for shelter. Sparks met him by ramming the shotgun's double barrels into his belly. As the Indian bent over, the old man drove the butt of the greener against his skull, shattering it. But then the third man reached Sparks and drove a knife into his side. Sparks yelled in pain, got a hand on the Kiowa's throat, twisted, throwing both of them to the ground. With his other hand, Sparks ripped the blade from his own body and began using it against its owner. He drove the knife into the Kiowa's chest three times before he collapsed over the warrior he had just killed.

Meanwhile, Washburn reversed his grip on the Spencer since there was no more time to reload. Holding the barrel and using it as a club, he flailed around him as several of the Indians swarmed him. A bullet took Washburn in the thigh, making his leg collapse underneath him. He fought on, jabbing the Spencer's jaggedly broken stock into the face of one of the Kiowas. Dropping the rifle, Washburn fumbled out his pistol and emptied it. Two more of the warriors fell to the onslaught. Another one was about to blow Washburn's brains out when Fargo saw what was happening. His hand streaked to his Colt, and the heavy revolver bucked in his hand as he blasted a hole through the Kiowa's body.

Then Fargo swiveled back toward the warriors who were leaping at him and Susannah. She shot one of them through the throat, then coolly put a bullet into the belly of another. Fargo gunned down one man with the Colt, then suddenly found himself grappling hand to hand with another. He dropped the revolver, stooped, and came up with the Arkansas toothpick. The razor-sharp blade ripped into the man's belly, opening it so that his intestines spilled out. Fargo shoved the dying man away and turned, looking for the next threat he had to meet, when he heard Susannah scream.

Fargo whirled toward her and got a shock when he saw that Tree That Burns was standing over her, his hands free. Another Kiowa warrior was with the chief, and Fargo realized that the man must have slipped past them and slashed the bonds on the prisoner's wrists. Tree That Burns was leaning over, poised to plunge a knife into Susannah's body.

Fargo acted instinctively, his arm whipping up and back, then forward. The Arkansas toothpick flashed through the air and embedded itself in the war chief's chest with a thud. Tree That Burns staggered back a step and looked down in disbelief at the handle of the knife protruding from his chest. Then his eyes rolled up in his head and he pitched to the side.

Fargo dived forward, crashing into the warrior who had freed Tree That Burns. Both of them went down, with Fargo landing on top. The Indian jerked violently and then went limp underneath Fargo, and the Trailsman saw that the man's head had landed on a rock. The impact must have shattered his skull. Blood and gray matter began to drip down the rock on which the back of his head rested.

Fargo rolled off the corpse and grabbed the Colt he had dropped a moment earlier. He came up on his knees and lifted the gun, his thumb looped around the hammer, ready to fire.

There was nothing to shoot at. Silence settled down on

the hilltop, broken only by the now-faint keening of the wind through the cave.

Fargo drew in a deep, ragged breath as he looked around. Bodies lay scattered everywhere, mute testament to the carnage that had taken place here. There was life among the devastation, however. Susannah climbed slowly to her feet and came toward Fargo. She was splashed with blood, but she seemed to be moving all right. The blood wasn't hers.

A few feet away, Washburn was sitting up, his back propped against a rock. He was reloading his six-gun. He grinned wearily at Fargo, who asked, "How are you, Paul?"

"They blowed my leg out from under me, but I reckon I'll live. Don't worry about me, Fargo. Go check on Sparks."

Fargo walked over to the old man, who still lay atop the last Indian he had killed. His fingers were still locked around the handle of the knife he had driven into the Kiowa's chest.

Carefully, Fargo rolled Sparks off the corpse. The side of the old man's shirt was soaked with blood, but he was breathing.

Susannah knelt beside Fargo. "I'll tend to him," she said.

Fargo nodded. He needed to check on the rest of the war party. He stood, picked up the Henry, chambered a round, and went from body to body. All of the Kiowas were dead, including Tree That Burns.

It was hard to believe. When people heard that the four of them had not only held off the much larger party of Kiowas—not only held them off but wiped them out—the story would probably take on an epic quality as it was repeated and passed on throughout the frontier. Battles like this became the stuff of myth and legend, and in the telling they took on a shining quality that was totally absent from the real thing: a few minutes of terror and chaos, with the sound of gunshots hammering the ears and the stench of burned powder and spilled blood filling the nostrils. Tiredly, Fargo scrubbed a hand over his bearded face.

"I think if I can stop the bleeding, Sparks will be all right," Susannah said. "Then I'll tie up that wound on Mr. Washburn's leg."

"Don't fret about me," Washburn said. "It'll take more'n

a scratch like this to put me under." He looked at the body of Tree That Burns. "Looks like the chief didn't make it."

"No," Fargo said. "It turned out to be his own death song he was singing, after all."

# 15

Fargo and his companions spent the rest of that day and that night just inside the hillside cave. He and Susannah helped Washburn and Sparks into the cave, then cleaned and bandaged the wounds of the two older men. Sparks had a deep gash in his side, but Fargo thought that the blade hadn't reached the old man's vitals. Likewise, the bullet that had caught Washburn in the thigh had passed cleanly, without breaking the bone. Both men would heal as long as their wounds stayed clean and didn't fester.

Once Washburn and Sparks were resting comfortably and Fargo had rounded up the Ovaro and the other horses, Fargo and Susannah set out to tend to the bodies of the Kiowas. The two of them couldn't dig a mass grave big enough for all the corpses, but there was a shallow ravine nearby that would serve. Fargo dragged the bodies there and dumped them over the edge, then he and Susannah covered them with rocks and finally collapsed the bank of the ravine down over them, covering the rocks with dirt. It was the best they could do. Fargo felt no liking or sympathy for the members of the war party, but he accorded them some grudging respect, especially Tree That Burns. The war chief, though cold-blooded and ruthless, had possessed courage.

That done, Fargo and Susannah went back to the cave. Fargo built a small fire, and later, he and Susannah slept in each other's arms next to its embers.

Fargo woke the next morning with Susannah snuggled against him, her hand at his groin, stroking and caressing.

His shaft was hard as she manipulated it through his trousers. Fargo kissed her lightly and said, "Later."

"I know," she whispered. "There'll be plenty of time."

Washburn and Sparks were stirring. After breakfast, the two of them hobbled out of the cave, supporting each other. Sparks glanced at the knoll where the battle had taken place and said, "Hell of a fight, weren't it?"

"I reckon folks'll be talkin' about it for a while," Washburn agreed.

"Somebody ought to put up some sort o' marker tellin' about it, so when there's a road runnin' through here, folks can stop and read about what happened."

"That's a mighty fine idea. We ought to see about doin' that. I could build a sign . . ."

Fargo saddled the horses and helped Washburn and Sparks mount up. Susannah was already in the saddle, and Sparks settled down behind her with a grin. Fargo swung onto the Ovaro's back and took the lead, heading for Fort Phantom Hill once more.

Later that day, they climbed the tallest hill they had yet encountered in this part of the country, an escarpment of sorts, and when they reached the top Fargo reined in and looked behind them. He could see for miles out across the Palo Pinto Hills. From up here, the dark valleys were no longer visible. Instead he saw a beautiful land of trees and streams, and to the south, richly grassed prairie dotted with post oaks and sand roughs. Sparks was right: Someday this country would all be settled.

Despite his aches and pains, Fargo was glad he had gotten to see it while it was still wild.

At the top of the hill, the land leveled out into a long plain with fewer trees and hills that were shallower and more rolling. Fargo knew that this terrain ran all the way to the Cap Rock, a hundred miles or more to the east. Beyond that was the southern edge of what some people called the Great American Desert, although Fargo had been across those plains and knew them to be teeming with life, not desert at all.

He wouldn't be going that far this time. Fort Phantom Hill was within a day's ride. They would have to spend one more night on the trail, but that was all.

Fargo had lost track of the days. He wasn't sure how long it had been since he and Washburn and Sparks had left Fort Worth, but he was sure the week that Major Gilmore had given Washburn was past. While they were camped that night, he brought up the subject of the government freight contract.

"Don't see how I can get it now," Washburn said. "I didn't make the deadline. Hell, I lost the whole wagon full of supplies."

"Through no fault of your own," Fargo pointed out. "Besides, your competition is Isaac Reese, and the army isn't going to deal with him when they find out he's been selling guns to the Indians."

Fargo glanced at Susannah as he spoke. She was staring stonily into the small fire that Fargo had built. He hated to talk so bluntly about her father, but there was no getting around it. Reese was a murderer and a renegade, and he had to be brought to justice, no matter what Susannah thought.

"You know, you're right," Washburn replied slowly, nodding as he thought about what Fargo had said. "I might have a chance at that contract after all."

"The soldier boys would be fools not to give it to you," Sparks said. "And once you've got it, I figure you'll want to hire me on as a driver."

Washburn grinned and extended a hand. "You've got the job," he said as he shook with Sparks.

Fargo was nodding in satisfaction as he heard horses approaching the camp. He stiffened, his hand going to the butt of the Colt. He didn't expect to run into another war party this close to the fort, but anything was possible on the frontier. Washburn and Sparks heard the hoofbeats, too, and reached for their guns.

"Hello the camp!"

Fargo recognized the voice that came out of the darkness. So did Susannah. Her head jerked up, and she half whispered, "Pa . . ."

"Come on in!" Fargo called. With the clip-clop of hooves, Isaac Reese rode in from the night. His son Malachi was with him. They were riding two of the horses from the bunch that had been left behind after the Kiowa war party jumped them.

Reese reined in and breathed, "My God," as he looked across the fire at Susannah. "You really got her back."

Susannah lifted her eyes to meet his gaze. "Hello, Pa," she said. "Hello, Malachi."

Reese swung down from the saddle and dropped the reins. He came around the fire, his arms extended. "Come here, gal," he said hoarsely.

Susannah stood up, her movements hesitant. For a second Fargo thought she was going to bolt rather than let her father hug her. But she stood there stiffly, submitting to Reese's embrace.

Reese must have felt her reaction, because he stepped back. With his left hand on her shoulder, he asked, "What's wrong, Susannah?"

"What do you think is wrong?" she snapped. "I was captured by those Indians."

"But now you're back, safe and sound. I'm sorry for what you went through, gal. I'm mighty glad Fargo was able to find you and get you away from those savages." Reese looked over his shoulder at Fargo. "I'm much obliged for the life of my girl. Mal and I would've come after you to help, but we had to lay up for a few days and rest those wounds we got in the fight with the Kiowas."

"Looks like you're better now," Fargo said.

"Reckon we'll live."

"Live to hang," Susannah spat.

Reese's head jerked back toward her. "What? What did you say?"

"I know all about it, Pa," Susannah went on, her voice shaking. "I know how you've been selling guns to the Indians. I even know how you cheated them by giving them defective rifles. You'll do anything for money, won't you? Anything! Even selling guns to the same sort of savages who . . . who killed my mother—!"

Susannah tried to pull away from him, but his hand tightened on her shoulder and yanked her toward him. At the same time, his right hand went under his duster, and as he spun toward Fargo it emerged holding a revolver. Fargo came sharply to his feet, but he couldn't draw and fire because Reese was holding Susannah in front of him as a shield.

Still mounted, Malachi had drawn his gun, too, and was

154

covering Washburn and Sparks. "Don't try anything, you old codgers," he warned them.

Reese locked eyes with Fargo. "We've been keeping an eye out for you, Fargo," he said as he leveled his gun at the Trailsman. "I figured that if you got back alive from chasing after those Kiowas, you'd know about my dealings with them. What did you do, talk to Tree That Burns? That red son of a bitch."

"At least he's honest about who he hates," Fargo grated.

"Hell, so am I. I planned to kill you boys anyway, if the Kiowas didn't." Reese glanced over at Susannah, who stood tautly in front of him. He had slipped his arm around her neck so that he could hold her more securely. "Didn't figure you'd turn my own daughter against me, though. Damn it, gal, don't you know that family counts for more than anything else?"

"Is that why you do business with the people who murdered my mother?"

"Never you mind who I do business with. That's *my* business." Reese glowered over the barrel of his gun at Fargo. "Reckon we'd better finish you off, so you won't go telling tales to the army. I still want that freight contract." The barrel of the revolver came up slightly as Reese's finger tightened on the trigger.

"Noooo!" Susannah howled. She lashed backward, her fist driving into Reese's groin. He yelled in pain and fired the gun in his hand, but his arm had jerked up a little and the bullet went high over Fargo's head.

Malachi triggered a shot, too, but Washburn and Sparks had already thrown themselves in different directions. The slug screamed harmlessly between them.

Fargo barreled forward as Susannah grabbed her father's arm and struggled with him. Reese jerked free and whipped the gun across her face, but before he could turn the barrel back toward Fargo, the Trailsman slammed into him. Reese went over backward.

They rolled through the edge of the fire, scattering the burning brands and sending sparks dancing into the air. Fargo had hold of Reese's wrist. He tried to shake Reese's grip on the gun but was unable to. The best Fargo could do was keep the barrel pointed away from him.

On the other side of the fire, Washburn rolled over and

came up with his six-gun. At the same moment, Sparks leveled the greener. Malachi didn't know which way to turn. Both of the older men fired at the same time. Washburn's bullet bored through Malachi's chest an instant before the charge of buckshot pitched him out of the saddle.

Reese threw a left that clipped Fargo's head and rocked him to the side. That allowed Reese to buck wildly and throw Fargo off of him. Reese came to his feet brandishing the gun and was about to shoot when, from the side, Susannah thrust a burning branch from the fire into his face. Reese screamed and staggered back, twisting toward Susannah and firing instinctively. The bullet caught her in the body and threw her backward like a giant fist.

"Susannah!" Fargo bellowed. He had come to one knee and had his gun out. He and Reese fired at the same time as Reese swiveled toward him. Reese's slug whipped past Fargo's head, but Fargo's bullet dug deeply into the other man's guts. Fargo triggered again and then again, each bullet driving Reese back another step as they smashed into him. Somehow Reese stayed on his feet and even tried to bring his gun in line for another shot. Fargo's Colt blasted again, and this time a black hole appeared in the center of Reese's forehead. He crashed to the ground and didn't move.

Fargo leaped to his feet and raced over to Susannah, who lay crumpled on the ground a few feet away. He dropped to his knees beside her and cradled her head in his lap. "Susannah!" he said urgently. "Susannah!"

Her eyes were closed, and the side of her shirt was soaked with blood. As Fargo held her, her eyelids flickered open. She stared up at him. Her eyes were large and dark in the pallor of her face. "Fargo . . . ?"

"You're going to be all right," Fargo told her. "Just hang on, Susannah. You're going to be all right . . ."

He believed what he was saying.

They had come too far, been through too much, for him not to believe now.

"You thought I was going to die."
"Nope."
"Sure you did. How could you not think so? I was bleeding like a stuck pig."

"I know a scratch when I see one," Fargo said.

Susannah punched him lightly on the shoulder. "The hell you say! You were convinced I wasn't going to make it."

Fargo shook his head stubbornly.

Susannah sighed and rested her head on his shoulder as they lay snuggled in the bedroll they were sharing under the star-dappled Texas sky. "Oh well," she said. "I suppose it's not worth arguing about." Her hand strayed to his manhood, which began to harden as soon as she wrapped her warm fingers around it. "Especially when there are so many more pleasant things to do."

"Better be careful," Fargo warned her. "You don't want to overexert yourself. Remember, that army surgeon at Fort Phantom Hill said it would take several weeks for that crease on your side to heal completely."

"What about you?" she demanded. "You've got gashes and bullet creases all over you."

"I'm used to it."

"Nobody ever gets used to bring shot and stabbed."

Fargo laughed. "Well, then, I reckon we'd better just be gentle with each other."

She eased atop him, warmly nude in his arms, and straddled his hips so that his rigid shaft slipped into her. "Ahhh," she breathed. Her hips began to move slowly. "Gentle. Like this?"

"Exactly like that," Fargo said.

Truth to tell, they had been taking it easy ever since leaving Fort Phantom Hill a week earlier, bound for San Antonio where Susannah's aunt, her only remaining relative, lived. Susannah planned to stay with her aunt for a spell while she made up her mind what she was going to do next.

Major Gilmore had been very interested in what Susannah had to say, just as Fargo had thought he would be. Once her wound had been treated by the post surgeon, she had explained to Gilmore about her father's dealings with the Indians and how Reese's murderous attacks had kept Paul Washburn from reaching the fort in the allotted time. Under the circumstances, Gilmore had assured Washburn that the government contract would be awarded to him, and Washburn and Sparks had remained at the fort to begin the work of setting up the supply line. When they returned to Fort Worth, they would be accompanied by a cavalry patrol.

"Sure hate to see you go," Washburn had said to Fargo before he and Susannah left the fort. "If you want to keep on workin' for me, I'd be mighty glad to have you."

"Oh, I reckon I'll drift on. I told Susannah I'd take her to San Antonio to see her aunt."

"Which trail are you takin'?" Sparks asked with a grin. "There's lots of ways to get to San Antonio. Some of 'em take longer'n others."

"Don't worry." Fargo grinned back at him. "I know just the trail I want."

Now, with Susannah lying atop him and gradually working her way to another climax, Fargo tightened his arms around her and brought her mouth to his. The kiss they shared was soft and tender, but it grew in urgency as the feelings inside them built. Fargo slid his hands down to her backside and held her steady as he drove up into her and began to spasm.

Nice and easy, all the way to San Antonio.

Skye Fargo sat astride his big Ovaro stallion and looked
up at the tall green pine trees along the trail outside of
Huntsville, Texas. Not so long ago, the trail had been used
mainly by the Indians, but now settlers were coming in with
their wagons. The trail was getting worn and rutted. Fargo
wasn't sure he approved of the change.

Somewhere back to the north of him was the state's
prison. Fargo had heard tales of the way things were there:
the tiny, dark cells that held three or four men, the brutal
guards who enjoyed beating the convicts, the food that
seemed almost alive because of the maggots that crawled
in it.

A hell of a place, Fargo thought, a lot different from a
peaceful trail among the towering pines with the cloudless
blue sky overhead. A man could feel mighty free and easy

on the trail, with money in his pocket from the last job he'd done and a little time on his hands. Fargo had both money and time, and he planned to ride down to the Gulf of Mexico and smell the tangy breeze again, maybe even take a swim in the salty water and taste it on his tongue.

A scream cut through the quiet air and shredded Fargo's pleasant thoughts. A hawk burst upward from one of the tallest pines and the tree top shook.

Fargo's lake-blue eyes narrowed and turned cold as ice. At first he thought the scream might have come from a panther, but the horse didn't turn a hair. Fargo knew that if a panther was around, the big horse would have shown some signs of nervousness.

When the scream came again, Fargo knew it was the scream of a woman, even before it was cut off as if someone had clamped a hand over the woman's mouth. Silence settled over everything, and the hawk circled above.

Fargo didn't like to go mixing in the problems of others, not knowing what the situation was, and he didn't like walking blindly into a situation that he knew nothing about. But the scream could have signaled distress. Someone could be in big trouble. It wasn't his trouble, not yet, but it paid for a man to be careful.

Shifting on the hand-tooled saddle of Mexican leather, Fargo eased the pinto on down the trail, looking at the tracks in the dirt. His keen eyes noted that at least three other horses had been there ahead of him that morning, and not long before. Fargo rode slowly, hoping to see where the other horses had left the trail and headed for the trees.

Before he reached that spot, however, he saw movement at the edge of the pines. The lower boughs shook, and a running figure burst out of the trees. Fargo was about a hundred yards away, but even at that distance he could tell that the figure was a woman because of the way she ran. She was wearing men's clothing, including a red-and-white shirt. Her long, dark hair was tied back in a thick braid that bounced up from her neck with every step she took. She was tall and lithe, and she ran easily, taking long strides through the tall grass that rippled in the slight breeze.

Pursuing her was a short, heavyset man whose thick legs pumped with the effort of each step, as he tried to keep up. He laughed as he ran. Then he called to the woman, who ignored him. He ran clumsily, as if under a strain, and he was losing ground with every step until the woman stumbled. She lunged forward and almost fell. She caught herself instantly, and after staggering for several yards, she recovered her form. But by then, the man was almost within reach of her. He threw himself at her and managed to get a hand on her shirt. As he fell, he pulled her down into the long grass with him.

Fargo watched all this dispassionately. If a man and a woman wanted to play a little game of slap-and-tickle in the woods, that was all right with him. They'd probably taken a picnic lunch into the woods and then gotten a little frisky. The woman might have changed her mind, but Fargo couldn't be sure. He thought now that the scream might have been one of pleasure rather than distress, cut off with a kiss instead of a hand. He'd heard plenty of women cry out in pleasure, and you could never be sure what kind of sound they'd make. The two people rolling around in the grass would most likely be a little embarrassed to be caught at their game by a stranger, but that wasn't Fargo's problem. He touched his spurs gently to the pinto's flanks and started forward.

Just as he did, the woman screamed again. This time there was no doubt about it. She wasn't taking any pleasure in what was happening. No matter how things had begun, they'd turned ugly.

Fargo thought he'd better take a hand. It was one thing to let an innocent sex game get out of hand, but it was something else again to take a woman against her will. He rode to where the grass was thrashing near the trail and was about to dismount when a movement on the edge of the trees caught his eye. He turned in the saddle for a better look and saw someone else come out of the woods.

It was another man, and this one was riding a big black mare. The man held the reins in his left hand and a pistol in his right. Fargo saw smoke puff from the pistol barrel and heard the blast. There was another shot, and he felt something hit his shoulder like the kick of a government mule, knocking him off the pinto and to the ground.

He landed on his back, his fall hardly cushioned by the grass, the air forced from his lungs by the impact. Gasping for breath, his head swimming, he nevertheless struggled to his feet, pulling the Colt from its holster at his side.

All the time he was thinking, *This is what comes of mixing in other people's trouble.*

He had the pistol up and cocked when the man who'd been chasing the woman hit him from behind, slamming into his back with a hard, broad shoulder, throwing him forward and down, and knocking the air out of him again.

Fargo hit the ground and rolled. Somehow he managed to hold on to the Colt, and this time he didn't even try to get up. When he came to a stop, he flopped over on his belly and snapped off a shot at the rider.

He missed, naturally enough. It was hard enough to hit a moving target if you were perfectly steady yourself, and it was damn near impossible after you'd been shot, fallen off a horse, been knocked down again, and rolled five yards.

Fargo stayed down, looking for the squat man, but he was nowhere to be seen. There was a scream from the woman, and Fargo figured the man had gone back to what he was doing, thinking that Fargo must be done for.

That was where he was wrong. Fargo stood up. His knees were a little weak, but they held him.

The rider was almost on him now. He had his gun aimed straight at Fargo, and he was too close to miss. But then so was Fargo, who pulled the trigger of the Colt twice.

The gun jumped in Fargo's hand and both bullets smacked into the rider's chest, throwing him out of the saddle. His horse kept on coming, however, and Fargo had to jump aside to avoid being run down. As he was picking himself up yet again, the squat man landed on his back.

Fargo tried to turn over, but the man held him flat. He smelled like unwashed flesh and bad whiskey, and he had a grip like iron. He got a forearm under Fargo's chin and tightened his hold, cutting off Fargo's air supply. With his other hand, he reached out and grabbed Fargo's wrist.

When he had a firm grip, he smashed Fargo's hand into the ground, trying to make him drop the Colt.

Fargo hung on. His lungs felt as if they were on fire, and he tried to suck air into them. It was as if his throat were caught in a vise, but he didn't let go of the pistol.

The man lowered his head and bit Fargo on the shoulder where he'd been shot.

A red haze filmed Fargo's vision. His fingers went limp, and the gun finally dropped to the ground. He couldn't breathe, and he didn't think he'd last much longer.

But then the iron grip on his neck loosened. The weight rolled off his back. Fargo sucked air and dust into his raw throat. He coughed, breathed again, and coughed some more.

When he could sit up, he saw that the squat man was standing a couple of feet away. The woman he'd been chasing was also standing nearby. She had Fargo's Colt, and she was pointing it at the man who'd been chasing her.

"Don't move, Mr. Powell," she told him. "If you do, I'll kill you."

"I don't think so," Powell said. His voice was surprisingly high for a man built like a barrel with legs. "I don't think you'd want to hurt a man just for tryin' to have a little fun."

"Maybe you thought it would be fun," the woman said. "I didn't. Maybe I should just kill you anyway."

That sounded like a damned good idea to Fargo. Powell was quick, and he was tricky. Best to kill him where he stood before he got the upper hand again.

Fargo opened his mouth to say so, but no words came out. Instead he made a sound a little like the cawing of a tired old crow.

The sound was just enough to distract the woman, whose eyes drifted off Powell's face for less than a second, which was all the time that Powell needed. Quick as a cat, he sprang for her, slapping the pistol from her hand and putting a shoulder into her chest. He was about to make a grab for the pistol when he turned to check on Fargo, who had crawled over to the big Ovaro and pulled himself upright. He was trying to slide the big Henry rifle from the scabbard, so Powell left the pistol where it was lying, ran to the black mare, and pulled himself into the saddle. He slapped the reins and dug in his heels. The big black horse jumped forward and broke into a run.

Fargo got the Henry out, but he didn't bother to shoot. He was still winded and shaken not to mention shot and bitten. Shooting at Powell would just be wasting a bullet.

He slid the rifle back into the scabbard and leaned against the pinto. The woman was standing over the man Fargo had shot, pointing the pistol down at his head.

"Don't waste the bullet," Fargo croaked. "He won't get any deader."

The woman held the pistol steady for a while. Then she nodded and moved it, holding it down by her leg.

"Are you all right?" she asked.

Fargo managed a grin. His throat was feeling better, but his voice still came out sounding like a frog with pneumonia.

"Do I look all right?" he said.

The woman gave him an appraising look with her big black eyes, and he looked right back. She was a fine figure of a woman, nearly as tall as Fargo himself, and she had proud high breasts that her loose man's shirt couldn't hide. Her cotton denim pants fit her in a way that emphasized the curve of her hips and her fine, tight rump. Her lips were a little too full, and her sensuous mouth a little too wide, but she was a beauty, all right. No mistaking that.

"You'll do," she said.

"So will you," Fargo croaked.

"What's that supposed to mean?"

"Whatever you want it to," Fargo said, his voice already getting stronger. "Who were those two men, and what the hell was going on here?"

"It's a long story."

"I have time."

"You certainly do. You're not going anywhere for a while, not with that shoulder wound."

"I'm not worried so much about the wound," Fargo said. "What I'm worried about is the bite."

"Bite?"

"That fella you called Powell bit me right where I was shot."

"A man's mouth is dirtier than a dog's," the woman said. "We have to get that wound cleaned out. Can you get on that horse?"

"I think so," Fargo said.

"Then do it and follow me."

She handed Fargo his pistol and started walking toward the trees without looking back. Fargo stood beside the pinto for a moment, watching her. Then he pulled himself up into the saddle.

"What's your name?" he called after her.

The woman didn't stop walking. She didn't even look back.

"Jezebel," she said. "Jezebel Carson."

"Nice name," Fargo said.

This time, Jezebel Carson didn't answer. She just kept on making long strides toward the pines.

For a couple of seconds, Fargo admired the way her backside worked inside the tight pants. Then he clucked to the pinto and followed her.

*No other series has this much historical action!*

# THE TRAILSMAN

| | | |
|---|---|---|
| ❏ #211: | BADLANDS BLOODBATH | 0-451-19694-5 |
| ❏ #212: | SIOUX STAMPEDE | 0-451-19757-7 |
| ❏ #214: | TEXAS HELLION | 0-451-19758-5 |
| ❏ #215: | DUET FOR SIX-GUNS | 0-451-19866-2 |
| ❏ #216: | HIGH SIERRA HORROR | 0-451-19860-3 |
| ❏ #217: | DAKOTA DECEPTION | 0-451-19759-3 |
| ❏ #218: | PECOS BELLE BRIGADE | 0-451-19891-3 |
| ❏ #219: | ARIZONA SILVER STRIKE | 0-451-19932-4 |
| ❏ #220: | MONTANA GUN SHARPS | 0-451-19964-2 |
| ❏ #221: | CALIFORNIA CRUSADER | 0-451-19977-4 |
| ❏ #223: | IDAHO GHOST-TOWN | 0-451-20024-1 |
| ❏ #224: | TEXAS TINHORNS | 0-451-20041-1 |
| ❏ #225: | PRAIRIE FIRESTORM | 0-451-20072-1 |
| ❏ #226: | NEBRASKA SLAYING GROUND | 0-451-20097-7 |
| ❏ #227: | NAVAJO REVENGE | 0-451-20133-7 |
| ❏ #228: | WYOMING WAR CRY | 0-451-20148-5 |
| ❏ #229: | MANITOBA MARAUDERS | 0-451-20164-7 |
| ❏ #230: | FLATWATER FIREBRAND | 0-451-20202-3 |
| ❏ #231: | SALT LAKE SIREN | 0-451-20222-8 |
| ❏ #234: | APACHE DUEL | 0-451-20281-3 |
| ❏ #235: | FLATHEAD FURY | 0-451-20298-8 |
| ❏ #237: | DAKOTA DAMNATION | 0-451-20372-0 |
| ❏ #238: | CHEROKEE JUSTICE | 0-451-20403-4 |
| ❏ #239: | COMANCHE BATTLE CRY | 0-451-20423-9 |
| ❏ #240: | FRISCO FILLY | 0-451-20442-5 |
| ❏ #241: | TEXAS BLOOD MONEY | 0-451-20466-2 |

To order call: 1-800-788-6262

S310